BOBBY ★ VS. ★ GIRLS (ACCIDENTALLY)

LISA YEE

ILLUSTRATED BY
★★★ DAN ★★★ SANTAT

SCHOLASTIC INC.
New York   Toronto   London   Auckland
Sydney   Mexico City   New Delhi   Hong Kong

★ **For Benny** ★

No part of this publication may be reproduced, stored in a retrieval system, or transmitted in any form or by any means, electronic, mechanical, photocopying, recording, or otherwise, without written permission of the publisher. For information regarding permission, write to: Scholastic Inc., Attention: Permissions Department, 557 Broadway, New York, New York 10012.

ISBN-13: 978-0-545-19749-6
ISBN-10: 0-545-19749-X

Arthur A. Levine Books hardcover edition published by Arthur A. Levine Books, an imprint of Scholastic Inc., September 2009

10 9 8 7 6 5 4 3 2 1   9 10 11 12 13 14/0
Printed in the U.S.A.   40
First Scholastic paperback printing, September 2009

★★★ TABLE OF CONTENTS ★★★

★ ★

★★★ CHAPTER 1 ★★★

The Fish and the Fiesta

The Ellis-Chan family heard the screams before they even entered Wild Acres Amusement Park. Once inside, all five of them tilted their heads back and looked up. Casey covered her ears. Annie broke into a grin. Mr. and Mrs. Ellis-Chan held hands. And Bobby wondered if anyone would notice if he ran away.

"Look!" Annie sounded awestruck. "It's Monstroso!"

Mr. Ellis-Chan glanced down at Bobby. "What do you say, son? Do you want to try it this year?"

Bobby swallowed hard as the cars of the giant roller coaster chugged up the rickety wooden rails. When they got to the very top, it was as if the world stood still for a split second before the riders plunged down Monstroso's death drop.

"Um, maybe later," Bobby croaked.

The whole town of Rancho Rosetta, California, turned out for the annual Labor Day Fiesta at Wild Acres. Bobby could hear a rock band playing in the distance as the riders exited Monstroso, laughing and giving each other high fives. Some people got right back in line to go on again. Bobby shook his head. The only ride worth going on over and over was the bumper cars. He also loved the Circus Train, but that was a little kid ride.

"Casey and I are going to KiddieLand," Mrs. Ellis-Chan declared.

"KiddieLand! KiddieLand!" Casey echoed. Her crown fell off as she hopped up and down, waving her wand in the air. "They have a bouncy castle in KiddieLand!"

"I'll keep an eye on Annie and Bobby," Mr. Ellis-Chan assured his wife.

"I don't need anyone to watch me," Annie protested. "I'm in high school, remember? I'm practically an adult!" She paused and adjusted her football helmet. "Dad, can I have some money? I want to play some games."

"Games!" Bobby jumped in. "That sounds like a good idea." Games were much more appealing than possibly dying on Monstroso. Plus, last year Bobby almost won a giraffe at the Spin-a-Wheel.

As Annie, Bobby, and their father made their way toward the games, people all around them froze with one arm out and then growled. Even though this happened all the time, Bobby didn't think he'd ever get used to it.

Mr. Ellis-Chan was a former linebacker with the Los Angeles Earthquakes pro football team. He had been nick-named "The Freezer" for his ability to stop his opponents cold in their tracks. Bobby's dad would dig in his heels, hold one hand straight out in front of him, and make such a ferocious noise that a sports announcer once declared it "the growl heard 'round the world."

Mr. Ellis-Chan was now retired. But even though he had traded in his football jersey to become a stay-at-home dad, many of the residents of Rancho Rosetta were thrilled to have an ex–football star living among them.

"Look!" Annie cried as they neared the Football Throw. "I'm going to win that giant panda!"

Annie played quarterback on the Rancho Rosetta High School football team. When she won the job, the headline in the local newspaper read, "Freezer's Daughter Follows in His

Footsteps." Mr. Ellis-Chan had been so proud that he burst into tears.

"Here, little lady." The man in the Football Throw booth handed Annie a ball. He winked at Bobby and whispered, "Girls can't throw."

Bobby glanced at his sister, who was staring steely-eyed at the tire hanging from a rope on the ceiling. When Annie's ball spiraled straight through the tire, the Football Throw man's smug smile fell off his face.

As football after football sailed through the tire, the Football Throw man sank down onto a stool in the corner of the booth. At last, Annie stopped. She looked at her father and asked, "Dad, do you want to go next?"

The Football Throw man stared at the huge figure looming before him and stammered, "You're . . . you're . . . you're The Freezer!"

Mr. Ellis-Chan smiled modestly, then turned to his son. "Bobby, do you want to give it a try before I go?"

Just as Bobby was trying to think up an excuse not to play, he heard a familiar voice calling, "Bobby! Bobby, over here!"

He spun around and broke into a grin when he spotted Holly Harper racing toward him. The two friends high-fived with their right hands, high-fived with their left hands, stuck their thumbs in their ears, wiggled their fingers, and then shouted "Whoop! Whoop! Whoop!" They had been doing this for as long as they could remember. At school Bobby tried to avoid Holly, since it was considered weird to have a friend who was a girl. But they were miles away from Rancho Rosetta Elementary.

"Bobby, I missed you!" Holly exclaimed. "How was your trip?"

They hadn't seen each other for a whole month. Holly had been on vacation with her family, and before she got back, Bobby had gone on the road with his grandparents.

"It was so great!" he said. "Grammy, Gramps, and I drove up and down the Pacific Coast Highway." He could picture his grandparents' shiny silver trailer being pulled by their battered red Jeep. "We visited Zuma Beach and Hearst Castle and went all the way up to Oregon! Here, I got something for you." Bobby dug around in his pockets. He fished out a worn piece of string and a nickel that had a hole in it before he found what he was looking for.

Holly eagerly examined the smooth reddish rock that Bobby handed to her. "Wowza! It's almost totally round, like a marble," she exclaimed. "This one's even better than the one I found in the Arroyo Seco last year."

Bobby nodded. "I thought you'd like it. I picked it up on the beach at Big Sur." Holly loved rocks almost as much as he did. "When we go to the Arroyo Seco tomorrow, let's look for rocks with funny shapes."

Holly hesitated. "Um, I can't go tomorrow."

"But we always go rock hunting the day before school starts," Bobby reminded her.

"I know," Holly said, refusing to meet his gaze. "But, well, I forgot and promised Jillian I'd go shopping with her. . . ." Her voice trailed off for a moment. "I know! We can go rock hunting next weekend."

Bobby shook his head. "It wouldn't be the same."

There was an awkward silence as Holly studied the rock and Bobby studied her. He didn't like it that she looked sad, but he also didn't like it that she had forgotten about their tradition. Something about Holly was different. It wasn't her freckles, which looked the same. He had always admired Holly's freckles. One time she even let him do a dot-to-dot on her face with a marker. (They both got in big trouble for that one.) But there was something else. . . .

Bobby stepped back. "Your h-h-h-hair!" he said, pointing. "It's all straight and shiny."

"Thanks," Holly said, flashing her familiar smile.

Holly used to have a tangle of brown hair that was big and bushy and perfect. She and Bobby could hide paper clips and plastic army men in it. Once they even put a frog in her hair to conceal it from Holly's mom. Bobby sighed. There was no way you could hide a frog in straight hair.

"Hooray!" someone shouted behind them.

"Thanks, Freezer!!"

"Woooooo woooooo!!!"

"Look!" Holly pointed over Bobby's shoulder. "Annie and your dad have a lot of fans." Sure enough, the mob around the Football Throw booth was cheering his dad and sister as they won prize after prize. The roar got even louder as they tossed some of their prizes into the crowd. The only person who didn't look happy was the Football Throw man.

Bobby had never won anything in his life, and he could barely throw a football, no matter how much his dad tried to teach him. He turned away as Annie won a stuffed giant panda. It was bigger than Casey. "Let's walk around," Bobby suggested. "We just have to be able to see my dad at all times."

"That won't be hard." Holly gestured to the group of adoring fans mobbing Mr. Ellis-Chan. When Bobby winced, she reassured him, "Remember, you're the one who gets to go home with him. He's your dad, not theirs."

She always could make him feel better.

Their first stop was the cotton candy booth, Holly's favorite. They watched with awe as the lady wove a huge web of spun sugar around a paper cone, so that it resembled a fluffy pink beehive. Holly pulled off a big piece of cotton candy and let it melt in her mouth.

Now it was Bobby's turn to decide where to go. As they hurried toward Marv's Marvelous Mini Donuts, he asked, "So why did you straighten your hair?"

"Jillian thought it would look better," Holly said. She offered Bobby some cotton candy, but he shook his head. "She even gave me some special shampoo that makes your hair straighter and shiny. Do you want to try it?"

"Why?" Bobby asked. "Is there something wrong with my hair?"

Holly just smiled. Bobby's thick, dark brown hair looked like a tornado had blown through it in twelve different directions. No amount of combing could tame it.

"There's nothing wrong with your hair if that's the way you like it," Holly assured him. "But Jillian offered to help me with mine and I let her."

"Since when did you start listening to Jillian Zarr?" Bobby asked.

"Well, when you were on vacation, Jillian invited me to a sleepover. And then I invited her to the movies, and we ended up spending a lot of time together. She's really nice once you get to know her."

Bobby shrugged. He had no desire to get to know Jillian Zarr.

As they continued walking, a wonderful scent led Bobby to his destination. Marv's Marvelous Mini Donuts were Bobby's favorite part of the Fiesta. A small group of people stood at the booth, watching the donuts being made. Bobby slipped up to the front. A metal tube dropped small perfect halos of dough into a vat of boiling oil. The donuts floated happily in the oil, turning golden brown as they made their way down to a rack that rose up and flipped them over so the other side could fry. When the donuts were done, the machine dropped them onto a cooling tray.

Bobby loved the smell of fresh donuts. He could practically taste them as the donut man sprinkled them with generous amounts of sugar and cinnamon, then popped them into brown paper sacks while they were still hot.

"I'll take six," Bobby called out. If he ever got rich, the first thing he'd buy would be his very own donut machine.

As they headed toward the game booths, Bobby happily munched on his donuts. Mr. Ellis-Chan was still entertaining his fans with stories about his football days. Annie ran by with her friends and yelled, "Hey, Squirt, look what I won!" She had the stuffed giant panda tucked under one arm and an enormous purple elephant under the other.

Holly finished her cotton candy and wiped her hands on her shorts. "How are the donuts, Bobby?"

Bobby peered into the bag. There was only one left. He looked at Holly and then he looked at the donut. Then he looked at Holly again; then he looked at the donut. "Do you want one?" he asked.

"No, thanks." Holly patted her stomach. "I'm full of cotton candy."

Bobby sighed with relief. As he savored the last donut, Holly stopped in front of a booth lined with balloons. "Let's try this."

"You go ahead. I'm still eating," Bobby said with his mouth full. He watched Holly try to pop the balloons with darts. She missed each time.

"Oh well. How about we do something else?" Holly said. "Maybe something easier."

Bobby pointed to the Coin Toss. "What about that?"

Players tossed coins into shallow glass bowls and plates. If one of your coins stayed in, you got to keep whatever object your coin landed in. The loud pinging sounded like music. Bobby wanted to win something nice like the yellow candy dish for his mother. But all of his and Holly's coins kept bouncing out. A few didn't even land near anything.

"Come on, let's go over there," Holly suggested, tugging on his sleeve.

The Goldfish Toss looked simple enough. All you had to do was throw a Ping-Pong ball into a goldfish bowl. If you made it, you got to keep the fish. "I don't think so," Bobby said. He only had a dollar left, and that was enough to buy three more mini donuts.

"Well, I'm going to try," Holly announced. She handed over her dollar in exchange for three Ping-Pong balls.

One. Two. Three. Holly missed each time.

"Want to try again?" the man said, holding out three more Ping-Pong balls. "You were pretty close that last time."

Holly bit her lip. "I don't have any money left," she said glumly.

Bobby could feel the dollar in his pocket.

"I was pretty close, though, wasn't I?" she asked him.

The mini donuts were awfully good. And Bobby got them only once a year. Holly's shoulders slumped as she started to walk away.

"Here!" Bobby held out his dollar. "Three Ping-Pong balls, please."

Holly perked up. "Bobby, are you going to play?"

He shook his head. "No, you are," he said, handing the balls to Holly.

Her eyes lit up. "Gee, thanks, Bobby!"

One.

Two.

Holly had one more chance left. Bobby crossed his fingers.

Three.

Bobby and Holly were both beaming as the man handed her the bowl. The orange goldfish looked scared.

"What are you going to name him?" Bobby asked.

"I don't know." Holly had to walk really slowly so the water wouldn't spill. "You decide."

"Why me? He's your fish. You won him."

"But it was your dollar," Holly insisted. "I want you to have him. You're always talking about getting a pet. Besides, I already have Lulu and she might get jealous." Lulu was Holly's lizard.

"But —" Bobby didn't want a fish. Fish were dumb. What he wanted was a black Labrador retriever, the best animal in the entire world.

Holly held the fishbowl out to him like it was filled with diamonds. She smiled broadly. "Really, Bobby, I want you to have the fish."

"Thanks, I guess," Bobby said. As he took the fishbowl, someone tapped Holly on the shoulder.

"Hi, Holly!" It was Jillian Zarr.

Bobby and Holly automatically stepped away from each other. It was dangerous to be spotted by someone from school.

"Benny, you weren't talking to Holly, were you?" Jillian Zarr asked, eyeing him suspiciously.

"My name's Bobby," he corrected her. "And, um, we just, er, happened to be standing near each other."

Jillian Zarr towered over Bobby. She was freakishly tall for someone who was nine years old. Even her pigtails looked intimidating.

"Hey, Holly, you left your sleeping bag at my house," Jillian Zarr said, turning her back to Bobby. "My mom says she'll drop it off later. Come on, let's go to the petting farm. They have the cutest baby goats!"

"Oh, that sounds like fun!" Holly looked at Bobby. "Doesn't that sound like fun?"

Jillian Zarr made a sour face. "Why are you even talking to a boy?"

"I just . . . I was being nice?" Holly said.

Bobby shook his head. "I couldn't go to the petting zoo even if I wanted to. I'm allergic to fur, and it could trigger my allergies, and that could trigger my asthma."

"T-M-I," Jillian Zarr cried, linking arms with Holly. "Too much information!"

Holly glanced over her shoulder as Jillian Zarr dragged her way. "Good-bye," she mouthed.

Bobby gave his friend a weak wave, then watched the girls disappear into the crowd, leaving him holding a goldfish.

CHAPTER 2

Meet Rover

Bobby sat cross-legged on his bed, reading his *Encyclopedia of Dogs*. His room was painted orange, but the walls were plastered with his drawings of Great Danes, Yorkshire terriers, and every size dog in between. On the bookshelf was a collage Holly had given him when they both turned nine on May twenty-first. They had been born on the same night in the same hospital. The collage had a picture of them as newborns in their clear plastic cribs, next to another photo where they sat side by side in their high chairs when they were toddlers. Then there was a snapshot from the Halloween when they dressed as Thing One and Thing Two from *The Cat in the Hat*, and Bobby's favorite photo, of the two of them hugging Pluto at Disneyland.

When Bobby looked up from his book, the goldfish was swimming in circles. He knew how it felt. Every year he and

Holly went rock hunting on the last day of summer vacation. But today Holly was shopping for new school clothes with Jillian Zarr. Bobby couldn't believe it. What kind of person would pick clothes shopping over rock hunting? Just last summer, it had been Holly's idea to roll down Skeleton Hill in a tire. Was she turning into a *girl*?

Casey pranced into Bobby's room and waved Wandee, her favorite wand, over the fish bowl. "I thought you said he was a goldfish."

"He is."

Casey studied the fish. "But he's not gold, he's orange."

Bobby ignored her and looked at the Labrador in his book. It said that Labs were dependable and obedient and fun.

"What's Fishy's name?" Casey asked.

"He doesn't have a name," Bobby said, without looking up. He was still puzzling over why someone would rather go shopping than rock hunting.

"Fishy should have a name," Casey mused. She tapped Wandee against her forehead. "I know! How about Pretty Fish Who Swims a Lot in a Small Bowl?"

"That's not a good name," Bobby said. He turned the page.

"How about Da-Da-Doo?" Casey said.

"It's taken," Bobby told her. Casey adored the TV show *Princess Becky's Planet*. She was always begging Bobby to watch it with her. Afterward, they'd pretend that Casey was the sparkly little princess who helped poor people, and Bobby was Da-Da-Doo, the pint-sized dragon who blew rainbow bubbles instead of fire.

"Then you think of a better name." Casey pouted.

Bobby put down his book. Da-Da-Doo was a perfectly fine name for a dragon, but it was a dumb name for a fish. He considered Shamu and Nemo, but those were already taken as well. Bobby had never had a pet before, unless you counted the ant farm Gramps had given him when he was little. But there were too many ants to give them each names. And besides, they all looked the same.

Bobby glanced back at his dog book. "Rover," he finally said. "The fish's name is Rover."

"That's a dog name," Casey said, giggling. "Silly!"

"I know, but I'll probably never get a dog," Bobby grumbled. He picked up the rose quartz rock Holly had given him for Christmas. "I'm stuck with a fish."

When Casey left, Bobby asked Mr. Huggums, "If you had a sorta-best friend who asked you to go rock hunting, you'd go, right?"

There was no answer, but Bobby was used to that. Mr. Huggums was the worn brown cloth dog that Grammy had made for him when he was a baby. Annie called Mr. Huggums a "wiener dog," but Bobby thought that sounded disrespectful. He always referred to Mr. Huggums as a dachshund. It had been years, well, months . . . well, weeks since Bobby had last slept with Mr. Huggums. When Grammy and Gramps took Bobby on vacation, he had left Mr. Huggums at home. Stuffed animals were for little kids.

Bobby put his rock back on the shelf and headed down to the kitchen, where Mr. Ellis-Chan was mixing cookie dough. His white apron was splattered with stains and he had flour on his face. "Hey, kiddo, want to lick the batter off the spoon?"

"No, thanks." Bobby shook his head. His father's cookie dough tasted like paste. Bobby and Holly had eaten paste when they were in preschool, so he knew what that was like. "Where is everyone?"

"Annie's at football practice. Your mom just took Casey to ballet. So it's just you and me. How about when I'm done we go to the Bow Wow Pet Shop? There's something special I want to get for you."

When his dad winked at him, Bobby's eyes grew big. Bobby loved looking at the Labrador puppies in the window of Bow Wow. Could it be . . . ? Maybe he was getting a dog!

Bobby pushed open the door to the Bow Wow Pet Shop and was greeted by a ferocious growl. When The Freezer growled back, Mr. Ed, the pet store owner, pumped his fist in the air and cheered.

Bobby wished his father would stop goofing off. He was glad his mother wasn't with them. Because of his asthma, there was no way she'd ever let him get a dog. His dad, on the other hand, always forgot the rules, like no more than one hour of television a day, early bedtime on school nights, and don't hold the children upside down.

Mr. Ellis-Chan began talking to Mr. Ed in a low voice. Both men kept glancing at Bobby. Mr. Ed's hair was white, but he looked young. Bobby admired the little mouse peeking out of his shirt pocket and the small bird perched on his shoulder. Finally Mr. Ed said, "Follow me, Bobby. I have just what you're looking for!"

Mr. Ed strode purposefully toward the Labrador puppies. Bobby's breath quickened, and his knees felt like rubber. The puppies looked like balls of fur, only cuter. Bobby wondered which was his. He hoped it was the black one jumping up and down and wagging his tail. As he stepped toward him, Mr. Ed called out, "Bobby, over here. What do you think of this one?"

Mr. Ed was smiling.

Mr. Ellis-Chan was smiling.

Bobby was speechless.

Finally he managed to stammer, "Th-that's not a dog. It's an aquarium."

Mr. Ed chuckled. "Quite perceptive. Yes, it is an aquarium, and one of the finest ones we have. This one's on special this weekend, so the castle and the scuba diver come with it. And if I can get your dad to pose for a photo in my store, I'll throw in a bag of colored rocks for free! Say, Bobby, does your fish have a name?"

"Rover," Bobby said numbly.

"Rover." Mr. Ed nodded his approval. "Well, Rover's going to love it. He's one lucky fish!"

That night, as Bobby reread his dog-eared copy of *The Care and Feeding of Your Puppy*, Rover silently swam back and

forth and explored his new home. If he had gotten the puppy, they'd be playing together right now, Bobby thought. The puppy would be chewing on his shoe and licking Bobby's face, and Bobby would hug him. He couldn't hug a fish.

His mother came into the room and peered into the aquarium. "Rover seems to really like the castle." Bobby nodded. The castle was nice. It even had a drawbridge. "You have a big day tomorrow," she said as she sat on the side of his bed.

Bobby scooted over. "Fourth grade," he said proudly.

"My son is a fourth grader?" Mrs. Ellis-Chan teased. She brushed the hair out of Bobby's eyes. "I've heard good things about your new teacher."

As his mother continued to talk, Bobby's mind wandered. He hoped she was right. Last year hadn't been so great. Bobby was convinced that Mrs. Woods, his third grade teacher, hated him. It was an accident that during P.E. he had kicked her instead of the soccer ball. But no matter how much Bobby apologized, he could tell that Mrs. Woods didn't believe him.

Then there was the issue with his name. His real name was Robert Carver Ellis-Chan, so Mrs. Woods always called him Robert. Bobby hated being called Robert, or Robby or

Rob or Bob. Instead he preferred Bobby. Just Bobby. He had asked Mrs. Woods to call him Bobby about a million times. His mother even wrote a note, explaining that all his friends and family called him Bobby.

Still, Mrs. Woods insisted on calling him Robert. So for the entire third grade Bobby wasn't even himself.

". . . and be sure to look for cars when you cross the street," Mrs. Ellis-Chan was saying. Bobby nodded as he struggled to keep his eyes open. "And don't talk to strangers." Before leaving, his mother tucked him in and kissed his forehead.

Bobby's Labrador night-light glowed in the corner of the room. From his bed he could see Rover. He got up and turned off the aquarium light. Then Bobby crawled back into bed and drifted off to sleep.

★★★ CHAPTER 3 ★★★

The Route to School

WAKE UP!!!"

Bobby dove under the covers to avoid getting bashed over the head again. He peeked out to see Casey adjusting her sparkly crown with one hand as she gripped Wandee with the other.

"Bob-beeeeee, wake up!"

With the blanket over his head, Bobby slowly stood up on the bed. "I am the ghost of Da-Da-Doo, and I'm going to eat you," he said in his deepest, scariest voice. He jumped up and down and shouted, "Prepare for your doom!"

Casey shrieked and ran down the hall, screaming, "There's a monster in Bobby's bed!"

Bobby smiled triumphantly. It worked every time.

"Well, Mr. Huggums," he told his cloth dog, "today's the first day of fourth grade. Yep, I'm in the big league now!"

Bobby started to walk down to breakfast, and then he remembered. He returned to his room. Rover was swimming at the top of the aquarium, as if waiting for his own breakfast. Bobby dropped a pinch of fish food into the tank before heading back downstairs.

The Ellis-Chans were already eating when Bobby slid into his seat. "What are those?" Annie asked, pointing to the flat brown blobs on her plate.

"Pancakes," Mr. Ellis-Chan said proudly. He was wearing a new blue apron. It still had its price tag on. "I made them from scratch."

Bobby glanced warily around the kitchen. It looked like something had exploded. Dirty pots and pans were everywhere. A pancake slowly slid down the refrigerator door.

"I loooove pancakes!" Casey squealed as she flung one across the table. Bobby tried to catch it but missed.

"Stop it!" Annie grumbled. She peeled the pancake off her football helmet.

"Sock," said Bobby as he poked at a pancake with his fork. It was hard.

"What?"

Bobby pointed to her shoulder. "Sock."

Annie sighed. "Oh, thanks." The sock made crackling noises as she removed it from her jersey. Their dad's biggest battle used to be the opposing football team. Now it was static cling.

"Take off your helmet, Annie," her mother said. Mrs. Ellis-Chan was wearing her peach-colored business suit. Bobby thought she looked like the pretty dentist in that commercial where people sang about clean teeth. Mrs. Ellis-Chan closed her eyes as she took her first sip of coffee.

"I need to wear my helmet!" Annie protested. "It's for protection."

Mrs. Ellis-Chan's eyes fluttered open, and for a moment she seemed startled to see everyone. "Don't be silly, Annie. There's nothing dangerous about breakfast."

Bobby and his sister exchanged glances.

After breakfast, Mrs. Ellis-Chan pulled a static-y sock off her suit, then kissed Bobby good-bye before grabbing her briefcase. She came up with new products for Go Girly Girl, Inc., the country's largest maker of sparkly items. "Good luck today," she told him before driving off.

A warm feeling rushed through Bobby as he reached for his new blue backpack. It was filled with promise — freshly sharpened pencils in a clear plastic case, a glue stick, three empty folders, a yellow ruler, and a notebook of college-ruled paper.

Mr. Ellis-Chan handed a piece of paper to his son. "You may need this," he said.

"It looks like a football diagram." Bobby turned the paper sideways to study it more closely. It was crammed with arrows and circles and little pictures of trees and houses — even the scary gray cat with extra toes who lived on the corner. Near the school was a stick figure of Mr. Kirby, the ancient crossing guard.

"Since it's your first time walking to school by yourself, I thought a game plan might come in handy," his father explained.

Bobby shook his head. "But, Dad, I don't need —"

Mr. Ellis-Chan's jaw locked as he extended one arm in his patented Freezer position. Bobby shoved the paper into his pocket. There was no arguing with The Freezer.

As he walked toward school, Bobby felt big and brave. Sure, he was allowed to go to Holly's and to his friend Chess's house on his own, but they both lived nearby. Rancho Rosetta Elementary School was ten blocks away.

"Hey, Bobby, wait up!" Holly was running to catch up to him.

Bobby stared at her in disbelief. "Why are you wearing that? It's not Halloween."

Holly smoothed the sleeve of her light blue dress. The big white bow around the waist reminded him of toilet paper. "It's new," she said proudly. "Do you like it?"

Bobby shook his head. "Nope."

"That's not a very nice thing to say!" Holly scrunched up her nose all funny, like a rabbit. "I got this yesterday when I went shopping with Jillian. She says it looks stylish."

Bobby grimaced, but before he could reply, Holly leaned toward him and whispered, "I think we're being followed!"

Slowly, Bobby turned around. His father was behind a palm tree that did little to hide him. Casey was standing nearby with her eyes clenched shut. Bobby knew she was thinking that if she couldn't see you, you couldn't see her. He pulled the crumpled diagram from his pocket. "My dad doesn't trust me to get to school by myself," he told Holly.

She nodded and pulled out her own piece of paper. "My mom gave this to me." Soon they were both laughing at his diagram and her map.

When they were about a block away from school, Holly and Bobby came to the Parting Place. Without saying a word, Bobby sped up and Holly slowed down so they wouldn't be seen together near school. They had played together every day in pre-K and asked to sit next to each other in kindergarten. Even in first grade, Bobby and Holly were still best friends in public and didn't care when other kids made fun of them. But that was long ago. They were older now. Things changed.

Mr. Kirby was waiting at the corner with his big red STOP sign. Under STOP he had added the word "war" in small letters. Bobby, Holly, and a few more kids joined him. When the cars stopped moving, the group circled tightly around Mr. Kirby and shuffled slowly across the street. Mr. Kirby looked like he was about a hundred years old, and no one wanted him to tip over and fall.

When he was safely in front of the school, Mr. Kirby said in his cool creaky voice, "Bobby, is that The Freezer in the bushes?"

Bobby felt his face heat up.

"Aw, don't fret," Mr. Kirby assured him. "On the first day of school, the plants are chock-full of parents."

Bobby glanced around. Sure enough, there were moms and dads hiding everywhere. He waved good-bye to his father and Casey and headed to fourth grade.

CHAPTER 4

Robert Carver Ellis-Chan?

As Bobby walked past his old classrooms, he smiled at the kindergartners. A lot of them looked scared. First and second grade were pretty good years for Bobby. But not third grade. Last year was the worst year of Bobby's entire school career. Mrs. Woods was always looking down her sharp nose and snarling, "Robert, pay attention and sit still!"

Sitting still was not his best subject. Drawing was, or so Bobby thought until the day Mrs. Woods said loudly, "Robert, you were supposed to draw a farm animal, not a dinosaur! I'm not sure why you have so much trouble following directions." Bobby could still feel his ears burn. It had been a horse, not a dinosaur.

When Bobby entered Room 15, his friend Chess sprang up like a jack-in-the-box. Chess's real name was Sanjay Kapur, but everyone called him Chess because he loved the game so much. "Bobby! You're over there." Chess pointed to a desk near the window. On blue construction paper was the name ROBERT.

Bobby saw that he was next to another friend of his, St. James. Last year, Mrs. Woods had a silver bell on her desk that she'd ring whenever someone misbehaved. St. James got the most rings. He got in trouble for all the things he did, and even for some things he didn't do.

School was never dull when St. James was around. As if to prove this, he started making loud pig noises punctuated by hee-haws.

Bobby's good mood evaporated when he saw who was sitting on his other side — Jillian Zarr. Her frown made it clear that she wasn't happy with the seating assignment either.

"Good morning, class!" Bobby took his seat and faced front. "I'm Mrs. Carlson." His teacher was tall, with short brown hair, and looked young, not like a mom. Her heels clicked when she walked around the room. As she passed by his desk, Bobby caught the smell of oranges. He loved oranges.

While Mrs. Carlson took attendance, Bobby checked out the room. The bulletin board featured photos of famous

people like Barack Obama, Albert Einstein, and Sally Ride, the first woman astronaut. Two blue beanbag chairs nestled in the corner between shelves so stuffed with books that they looked like they would burst. On the wall near the sink was a poster that read "VOTE AND BE HEARD!"

"Robert Carver Ellis-Chan?"

Huh? Bobby looked up.

"Robert Carver Ellis-Chan?" Mrs. Carlson repeated.

"HERE!" Bobby didn't mean to shout; it just came out that way. Luckily, Mrs. Carlson didn't seem to mind. She just nodded and checked his name off her list.

Mrs. Carlson told the class that they had a fun year planned. "We'll be going on a field trip to Huntington Gardens this month, and pretty soon we'll have an election for student council representative, plus later we'll be putting on a musical. We're also going to learn about California's Spanish missions and do some interesting art projects."

Then Mrs. Carlson shared some amazing things about herself, like that she had been to astronaut camp, had a German shepherd named Buddy, and could wiggle her ears. As the rest of the class tried to wiggle their ears, Bobby thought about Buddy. Police dogs were always German shepherds. He had seen a whole television show about this.

"Now I'd like to find out about you," Mrs. Carlson told her new students. "Did you do something neat this summer? What are you looking forward to this school year? Do you have a unique hobby? Who would like to go first?"

St. James started talking even though he hadn't been called on. "My mom threw away my entire collection of rubber rats," he complained. He pushed his hair off his face and imitated a rat by making his hands look like claws. "You should have heard her scream that time I hid them in the refrigerator."

"I learned to dive off the high board," Holly volunteered. Bobby's jaw dropped. Last summer both he and Holly had been afraid to even climb up to the high board. She must have learned while he was on vacation.

"I'm getting a dog," Chess boasted when it was his turn.

Bobby felt a twinge of jealousy. Why couldn't he be the one getting a dog? He only had a stupid fish.

"Robert?" Mrs. Carlson looked right at him. "We haven't heard from you yet. What would you like me to know about you?"

Robert? Bobby didn't know if he could stand another year of being Robert. In a rush he said, "My name is Bobby, not Robert. I don't even know who Robert is!"

Mrs. Carlson looked surprised by his outburst. Bobby slouched lower in his chair. He wished he could disappear into a cotton-candy cloud like Da-Da-Doo, the dragon.

"Bobby," Mrs. Carlson said slowly, as if testing the sound of it. "Bobby. Of course, I can call you Bobby. Tell me something interesting about yourself, Bobby." Mrs. Carlson smiled encouragingly.

Bobby considered telling her about his rock collection, but that didn't sound as exciting as it really was. Then he remembered that he had recently learned how to do "walk the dog" with his yo-yo. But he knew Chess could do that too, so it wasn't unique. Finally he said, "Uh, my father is The Freezer, the football player."

"That's very cool, Bobby." Mrs. Carlson nodded. "But I want to know something about *you*. For example, what do you like to do when you're alone?"

Bobby thought so hard his eyebrows almost touched. "Well, sometimes I practice writing my name. I try different lettering so it looks sort of fancy."

"I can tell that you're very artistic," Mrs. Carlson said. "We'll be painting murals soon. I'll bet you're going to be great at that!"

Bobby smiled. Fourth grade was a million times better than third grade.

MRS. CARLSON

★★★ CHAPTER 5 ★★★

Wilbur, the Finest Dog

The first week of school sped by. By Thursday afternoon, besides all their regular work, the students of Room 15 had learned how to say "hello" in five different languages: *ciao, shalom, nei hao, hola, jambo.* Plus, they found out why elections were important, and that teachers sometimes snorted when they laughed. Bobby liked Mrs. Carlson more every day.

"How's Rover?" Holly asked as they walked to school on Friday morning. She was munching on a Cinnamon Crunchy Toasty Oatsie cereal bar.

"Fine," Bobby answered. He gazed longingly at her Toasty Oatsie. He had choked down burnt French toast and runny eggs for breakfast.

"Well, is he doing anything new?"

"Holly, Rover is a fish," Bobby reminded her. "Not a dog. Fish are fish. They don't do anything but swim around."

Holly shrugged. "I don't know, maybe Rover has hidden talents." She popped the last of the Toasty Oatsie into her mouth.

"If he does anything special," Bobby assured her, "I'll be sure to tell you first."

The Parting Place was just ahead. This time Holly sped up and Bobby slowed down. They had to be careful. The other day they had almost run into St. James doing wheelies while riding his bike to school. St. James hated girls even more than he hated lima beans — and he really hated lima beans.

That afternoon, when Bobby's classmate Jackson was at the board adding up whole numbers, he made a strange burping noise. His eyes widened and then he opened his mouth and threw up his lunch — spaghetti. When St. James announced, "It looks like bloody worms," several students started screaming. Then another boy puked, and Bobby had to hold his nose with one hand and cover his mouth with the other.

"If anyone needs to step outside," Mrs. Carlson said calmly, "you have my permission."

All at once the entire class stampeded toward the door. That sort of excitement had never happened in Mrs. Woods's class.

After school, Bobby had permission to hang out with Chess. They decided to hop all the way to Chess's house in hopes of breaking the world record for hopping. But their attempt came to a quick end when they ran into Jillian Zarr and Holly hogging the sidewalk.

"Move," Chess said.

"You move," Jillian Zarr shot back. "We were here first."

"We're breaking a world record," Bobby said as he hopped up and down. It was getting tiring and they hadn't even gone one block.

"Really?" said Holly. She looked intrigued.

"Are you going to move or not?" Chess asked. He was out of breath.

"Or not," Jillian Zarr said. "Holly and I aren't budging, are we, Holly?"

"I guess not," she said, sounding uncertain.

Bobby's backpack was starting to get heavy. "Come on, Holly, move or else."

"Or else what?" Holly asked.

"Or else this!" Bobby yelled. To be funny, he threw his jacket at her.

"Ouch!" The zipper from the jacket had scratched Holly's face. "Bobby?!"

Before Bobby could apologize, Jillian Zarr was telling Holly, "See, I told you boys were mean. I don't know why you even bother to talk to that Bobby person. Let's get out of here."

Hopping for the world record didn't seem nearly as much fun as when they first started. After a while, Chess and Bobby gave up hopping and instead just jumped whenever the mood hit them. At first it bothered Bobby that Holly was mad at him, but he quickly forgot about the fight when Chess's new dog, Wilbur, ran over to greet them. Bobby's stomach made such a loud rumbling sound that Wilbur yelped and backed away.

"Sorry," Bobby apologized to the dog. "I didn't eat lunch." His father had packed a big bag of burnt cookies and a sandwich that smelled like butter pickles and old sneakers.

"Saffron can make you a peanut butter sandwich," Chess offered. Saffron was the college girl who was supposed to watch Chess after school, but instead mostly watched soap operas.

"As long as it's not the crunchy kind of peanut butter," Bobby said, making a face. St. James had once said that the crunchy parts were cockroaches. Bobby didn't believe him, but still . . . it was probably best to be safe.

They went into the house and said hello to Saffron, then waited for a commercial so she could fix Bobby his sandwich. As he sat on the porch and devoured it, Bobby watched Chess chase Wilbur. Then Wilbur chased Chess. Then they both ran in circles and started all over again.

Bobby's heart swelled with longing when he gazed at Wilbur. He had patches of fur missing and one leg seemed considerably shorter than the rest. Still, he could catch a Frisbee and chase squirrels. He came when you called him and stayed put when you told him to. Wilbur was the finest dog Bobby had ever met.

"What kind of dog is he?" Bobby yelled to his friend. He was guessing that Wilbur was a rare breed like an Akbash or even a Tyrolean Hound.

"A mutt," Chess answered. He slowed down and plucked some brown leaves from Wilbur's fur. "Mutts are good."

Bobby nodded. Mutts *were* good. After all, wasn't he a mutt? Mrs. Carlson had said that immigrants from all over the world helped create the United States, and America was a melting pot of many races. Bobby had scribbled an equation in his notebook:

$$1/2 \text{ Chinese}$$
$$+ \ 1/8 \text{ English}$$
$$+ \ 1/8 \text{ French}$$
$$+ \ 1/8 \text{ German}$$
$$\underline{+ \ 1/8 \text{ Not Sure}}$$
$$100\% \text{ Bobby}$$

"Why'd you name him Wilbur?" Bobby asked.

"Well, I wasn't about to name him Charlotte. So it was either Wilbur or Templeton, but that's the name of a rat," Chess explained. Bobby nodded. Mrs. Woods had read *Charlotte's Web* aloud to the class last year. Chess loved the story so much that his mother bought him his own copy of the book.

The boys watched Wilbur scratch behind his ears with his hind leg. It looked easy, but when they tried to scratch their own ears with their feet, they fell over.

"So you named him after a pig instead?" Bobby asked as he sat up.

"Wilbur's a phenomenal name," Chess said defensively. Though he was small, Chess loved using big words.

"If I ever got a dog," Bobby said, "I was going to name him Rover, but that's my fish's name. So now I think I'd name my dog Galileo instead." He pictured himself running on the beach in slow motion with Galileo at his side.

"How is Rover?" Chess asked.

"Okay," Bobby answered.

"Fish are cool," Chess said as he threw a tennis ball. It didn't go far. "Ichthyology can be interesting."

"Whatever." Bobby watched Wilbur drop the ball at Chess's feet. "I'd like to see Rover do that," he said. "All he does is swim around all day."

"Poor Rover," Chess said, shaking his head. "That must be awfully boring for him."

Bobby paused. He had never thought of that.

"Here," Chess said as he grabbed Wilbur. "Take him. He doesn't bite that hard."

Bobby shook his head. If he touched anything with fur, the wheezing would start, and he'd end up having another asthma attack. "Sorry, Wilbur," he apologized. "I can't. I'm allergic to fur."

Yet, when Wilbur drooled and looked up with his wet brown eyes, Bobby found it impossible to resist. The dog's tail wagged so fast it looked like a windshield wiper gone crazy. Bobby reached out a hand. . . .

"Da-Da-Doo, Da-Da-Doo, what about you?"

It was 4:30 P.M., so *Princess Becky's Planet* was blasting from the television. A steady mist of asthma medicine filled Bobby's nebulizer mask as he inhaled, exhaled, inhaled, exhaled. Bobby imagined that he was an astronaut as he listened to his own breathing.

Inhale, exhale, inhale, exhale.

The machine made a loud, comforting humming sound. Though Bobby hated his nebulizer, he also knew it helped him stop coughing and wheezing, and that if he sat still long enough, the medicine would make his chest stop aching.

Inhale, exhale.

Mr. Ellis-Chan whistled as he wandered into the living room. He had a roll of paper towels tucked under one arm like a football. Casey sat up on the ledge of the couch behind her brother. "Bobby, look! I have curlers. Want to play beauty shop?"

"No," he said.

Inhale, exhale, inhale.

"Okay! Here we go," Casey squealed as she began putting pink curlers in Bobby's hair.

"I said 'no,'" Bobby repeated as he tried to bat her away. But Casey could not be stopped, and he couldn't just get up and leave since he was still on his nebulizer — and it was plugged into the wall. Finally Bobby gave up and watched Princess Becky as his sister filled his hair with curlers.

Just as Da-Da-Doo was about to blow magical bubbles to stop the Terrible Teeny Tiny Trolls, the doorbell rang. Bobby didn't bother to take his eyes off of the television. It was probably Annie. She was always forgetting her key.

"Bobby?" Holly stood in the doorway, holding his jacket. "I think this belongs to you." Bobby couldn't tell if she was yelling to be heard over the nebulizer or if she was still mad at him. Holly had a Band-Aid on her face where the zipper had hit her.

Guilt tugged at him. Bobby said thank you, but he tripped over his tongue and it came out sounding like "sank woooo."

Holly giggled. "See you later, Bobby. I like your hair!"

Bobby tore off his nebulizer mask. Several curlers flew through the air. "Holly! I can explain!" he yelled, his voice rising. But it was too late. She was gone.

CHAPTER 6

Bad News Bobby

The next morning, Holly was waiting in front of her house for Bobby as usual. Much to his relief, she didn't look mad anymore, *and* she didn't mention the curlers.

"Another new dress?" Bobby asked. This one was lemon-colored and sported a flower that almost looked real.

"Thanks for noticing," Holly said. "Hey, did you bring that picture?"

Bobby pulled a photo out of his backpack. It was from Grammy and Gramps. They had finally gotten around to developing the film from their trip. In the photo, Bobby and his grandparents were all doing jumping jacks on a pier at Moro Bay. Bobby's eyes lingered on the picture.

"You miss them, don't you?" Holly asked.

"Yeah," Bobby admitted. He kicked a pebble into the street. There were some things he could tell Holly and not

Chess, like how much Grammy and Gramps meant to him. Chess hardly ever saw his grandparents, and when he did, he tried to get away from them. "They act like zombies and smell like them too," he insisted.

As Holly handed the photo back, Bobby noticed something odd. "Hey, Holly, what's with your hands?"

"Pink Bubblegum nail polish." Holly wiggled her fingers in his face.

Bobby shook his head. "No, no, no, no, no!" He wondered if she had been zombified. "What's happening to you?"

Holly stopped walking. "Bobby, why are you getting all weird? It's just nail polish. Sheesh!"

"Dresses? Nail polish? Your hair?" he protested. "If you're not careful, you'll turn into a girl!"

Instead of thanking him for the warning, Holly balled up her fist and brought it inches away from Bobby's face. He couldn't see her nail polish anymore. Her eyes narrowed and her nose scrunched. "For your information, Robert, I am a girl!"

They walked to the Parting Place in silence as Bobby tried to figure out what had just happened. All he had done was try to be helpful.

The next day, Bobby complimented Holly by telling her that her dress looked like an upside-down mushroom. Yet this only seemed to get her mad again. It didn't help that later St. James said it was "the color of poo" and Bobby laughed.

Later, in class, Mrs. Carlson put a poster of the solar system up on the wall. "Who can name all of the planets?" she asked as she pushed in the last thumbtack.

Bobby knew his planets backward, forward, and sideways, but as much as he wanted to answer, he couldn't bring himself to raise his hand. He hoped Mrs. Carlson would call on him. He tried to look smart and eager to answer the question.

St. James yelled, "Girls go to Jupiter to get more stupider!"

Half the class broke out laughing. The other half shot alien death stares at St. James.

Mrs. Carlson lowered her voice. "St. James, perhaps you'd like to apologize to the girls."

"Girls, girls, girls," St. James said. "I am so totally truly absolutely sorry." He covered his mouth in an unsuccessful attempt to hide his smirk.

Mrs. Carlson announced that the class would split up into groups to create murals of the solar system. A short time later the classroom was bustling. Colorful bottles of tempera paints came out of the supply closet and butcher paper unfurled across the floor. Bobby was in the Blue Group. He was in charge of Mars. It was his favorite planet. He imagined friendly Martians frolicking with their two-headed dogs.

Bobby poured a big glob of red paint into a paper cup and plunged his brush into it. It looked like a twister as he swirled it around. Swirling, swirling, swirling, faster, faster, faster. He looked around to see who else was having as much fun as he was, when —

"Look at my dress!" Holly cried. "You've ruined it!" Sure enough, red paint was splattered across the front of Holly's dress. Several girls crowded around her and started clucking like chickens. Before Bobby could say anything, Holly huffed away.

Jillian Zarr sidled up to him and wagged her finger in Bobby's face. "We're going to keep an eye on you," she threatened. "You're bad news!"

St. James slapped him on the back. "Bad News Bobby — I like that!"

At recess, St. James and Jackson joined Bobby and Chess as they ran in circles and tried to make themselves dizzy. After everyone had fallen down at least twice, Jackson suggested, "Let's play Arctic ice robots!"

"What's that?" Chess asked.

"You know," Jackson explained. "It's where we're frozen robots and can't move. We have to be as still as possible."

Bobby relished the challenge. The only time he was still on purpose was when he slept. But even then, every morning his sheets were tangled around him like he had been in battle — and lost. He noticed that Holly was nearby with Jillian Zarr and her friends. Last year in Mrs. Woods's class, Bobby did a report on wolves. He had learned that wolves were social creatures that traveled in packs and were rarely seen alone. The girls reminded Bobby of a wolf pack.

As the boys tried to be as still as statues, the girls circled, getting dangerously closer with each pass. Bobby was holding his left foot high in the air and his arms out to the side. He wanted to shout at them to stay away, but he was frozen, just like the rest of the guys.

Bobby saw Holly approaching him. She brushed past his foot, knocking him down accidentally-on-purpose. "Oops, sorry," she said, giggling. Jillian Zarr gave Holly a nod of approval.

"You are not sorry," Bobby grumbled as he got up. He would have won the Arctic ice robot contest; he was sure of that. "You did that on purpose!"

"Did not."

"Did so."

Bobby rubbed his elbow. Was he bleeding? "You should apologize," he said, scowling. His elbow really hurt.

"NO!" Holly yelled. Her intensity surprised him. "YOU should apologize!"

"For what?"

"For ruining my dress!" Holly looked like she was about to cry. "My grandma made this."

Her dress did look pretty bad, all splotched with red. Bobby started to say something, but St. James stepped in. "He doesn't owe you an apology. You owe him one for knocking him over on purpose!"

Holly straightened up. When had she gotten taller than Bobby? "Bobby's the one who owes me an apology. Or is he too dumb to say, 'I'm sorry'?"

"Yeah," Jillian Zarr jumped in. "Bobby, you're a wimp for not apologizing. You wimp, you big wimpy wimp! Why can't you be stronger like your dad, or even your sisters?"

This was just too much. "Jillian Zarr, you're nothing but a GIRL," Bobby shouted. "And you too, Holly! You're both dumb girls!"

Jillian Zarr shouted back so half the playground could hear, "Bobby, you're the girl! YOU WEAR PINK CURLERS!"

Bobby felt as if he had been punched in the stomach. He was so stunned he couldn't even speak.

Chess rushed to his defense. "Jillian Zarr, you're a dunderhead!"

"Yeah," St. James added, "whatever he said. Plus, you're a big liar. Bobby doesn't wear curlers. Liar, liar, liar! You're worse than a liar. You're . . . You're a . . . You're a booger-eating gorilla liar!"

That was all the boys needed to hear. They instantly switched from Arctic ice robots to gorillas. As they hopped around and pretended to eat their boogers, the girls fled, screaming.

"That showed them," St. James said as he tried to make his knuckles drag on the ground.

"Indubitably," Chess agreed.

While the guys congratulated one another, Bobby was silent. There was only one person who could have told Jillian Zarr about the curlers.

★★★ CHAPTER 7 ★★★

PTA Lady Dad

The next morning, Bobby skateboarded quickly past Holly's house. When he got to the Parting Place, he kept going as if it never existed. As if Holly never existed.

"We've got a couple of big events coming up," Mrs. Carlson announced as she shuffled through the papers on her desk. "Today we have a special assembly sponsored by the PTA, featuring Professor Science! And don't forget the student council rep election in a few weeks, and before that we have our field trip to Huntington Gardens." A cheer went up from both the boys and the girls. Mrs. Carlson smiled and passed out the yellow permission forms. "Your parents will need to fill this out. . . ."

Bobby thought Huntington Gardens sounded like the kind of place a dog would enjoy. He was still thinking about dogs as his class filed into the auditorium. Assemblies were always exciting because you got to be someplace else. Bobby noticed that all the boys from Room 15 sat in one row and all the girls sat in another, right in front of them.

"Stop kicking my chair!" a girl snarled at St. James.

"It wasn't me," St. James said, looking shocked. When she turned around, he kicked her chair again. Then all the other boys kicked the chairs in front of them. Holly looked back and glared at Bobby. He pretended not to see her.

"All eyes on me, please!" Principal Coun stood on the edge of the stage. "Before our special guest Professor Science explains the mysteries of the universe, our newest PTA Lady has a special announcement. . . ."

A few kids started giggling and soon the whole auditorium was roaring. Bobby had to crane his neck to see what was so funny. He gasped. As a large figure came onstage, Bobby quickly slumped in his seat and pulled his shirt over his head.

"Hello, everyone! I'm the newest PTA Lady! My name is Roy Ellis-Chan, but many of you know me as Bobby's dad, The Freezer. Where is my kid, anyway?" Bobby sank lower into his seat. "Oh well," Mr. Ellis-Chan continued, "I'm here to encourage all of you to buy homemade baked

goods from the PTA bake sale. I'll be manning the table with the other PTA Ladies after school starting on Monday. See you there!"

Like a turtle, Bobby poked his head out of his shirt to see if it was safe to come out. It wasn't — his father was still onstage. Before he left, he did his famous freeze and growled. The entire audience growled back, even Principal Coun.

Bobby couldn't remember a time when people weren't growling around him. And if that wasn't embarrassing enough, now this — his father was a PTA Lady.

After school, Bobby really needed someone to talk to. But who? Chess was bad at keeping secrets. Holly wasn't speaking to him. His mother was at work, and his father was the one who he wanted to talk about.

Bobby watched Rover swimming up and down with Diver Dave. "Hey Rover," Bobby called out. "Got a minute?" Rover headed toward his boy. For the longest time the two just stared at each other. Finally, Bobby began talking as Rover listened.

"It's weird," Bobby confided. "When my dad announced that he was a PTA Lady, everyone started laughing. I just wanted to disappear. Do you think I should say something to him or just pretend it doesn't bother me?" Rover swam near the top of the water, then dove to the bottom and back up again. "I'm not sure what you're saying," Bobby told him. Rover circled twice around the tank before coming back. Slowly, Bobby nodded, then cried, "I get it! You're saying I should circle around. Not be too direct. I know, how about I ask Dad about himself first? Then I tell him how I feel. Thanks, Rover, I'll let you know how it goes!" Bobby was surprised at how easy it was to talk to his fish.

Mr. Ellis-Chan was in the kitchen scrubbing the counter when Bobby sat down at the table. "Hey, Dad? How come you stay home and Mom works?"

His father peeled off his rubber gloves, pulled up a chair, and sat across from Bobby. "Well, you know, after Sam Benzoni busted my knee in the playoffs a couple years ago, I had to stop playing football." Mr. Ellis-Chan held out a plate of cookies. They looked like checker pieces — the black ones. "Sam's nickname was The Freight Train. I guess a Freezer

can't stop a Freight Train!" Bobby noticed that even though his father was laughing, he didn't look happy. "Then I had that job at The Locker Room, but, well, you know how that went too."

Bobby nodded. Mr. Ellis-Chan had been the celebrity spokesman for a sports superstore chain. He even appeared in several commercials doing his famous Freezer growl. Then *Sports Legends* magazine did an article called "Where Are They Now?" In it, The Freezer was quoted as saying, "I always shop at van Straaten's Sports Closet in Rancho Rosetta. It's a small local store and the service is great!"

For a whole month after The Locker Room fired him, Mr. Ellis-Chan just sat in his Laz-E-Guy recliner and watched the videotape of Sam Benzoni tackling him over and over again. It was Mrs. Ellis-Chan's idea that he become a stay-at-home dad. Except for the cooking and cleaning and laundry parts, he was excellent at it.

"Princess is still napping," Mr. Ellis-Chan reported when he returned from checking on Casey. He poured Bobby a second glass of milk and then chugged what was left in the carton. "Being a full-time father is harder than playing in the NFL. There's no boot camp for this. I'm still learning. Do you have any tips for me?"

Bobby wiped off his milk mustache with the back of his hand. "Um, maybe you can just make plain sandwiches for lunch, like creamy peanut butter, instead of the ones with faces."

His father's massive shoulders slumped. "You don't like my Sandwich Faces of the Famous?"

"They're really nice," Bobby assured him. "But not for school. They're too, um, distracting."

His dad nodded. "Okay. Anything else?"

"How about calling yourself a PTA Dad, instead of a PTA Lady?"

"I thought it was sort of funny, but I can be a PTA Dad just as easily," Mr. Ellis-Chan said, nodding again. "I'm trying my best, Bobby. If ever I start to mess up, you just tell me, okay?"

"Sure thing, Dad." Bobby choked down another cookie and grinned. It was the greatest feeling spending time with his father, just the guys, the boys, the dudes. . . .

"Daaaaad," Casey yelled from upstairs. "Daddeeeee!!!"

Mr. Ellis-Chan pushed the whole plate of cookies in front of Bobby. "Well, it sounds like Princess is awake. I enjoyed our talk."

"Anytime, Dad," Bobby began. "I think —"

Before he could finish, his father was already bounding up the stairs.

★★★ CHAPTER 8 ★★★

Wandee's Magic

Where does he pee?"

Bobby was practicing writing his name in fancy lettering and drawing a little picture of himself beside it.

"Where does who pee?" he asked. "Casey! Don't tap on the aquarium, you'll give Rover a headache."

"Where does Fishy-fish-fish pee?" Casey pointed Wandee at Rover. "I don't see a bathroom."

"He pees in the water."

"Eeewwwww!!!" Casey's eyes grew big and she threw Wandee in the air. "Fishy-fish-fish is gross! Fishy-fish-fish swims in pee-pee!" she shrieked as she ran down the hall.

Bobby looked into the aquarium. Rover was now swimming in and out of his castle. Bobby dropped a pinch of fish food into the water. Immediately, Rover surfaced and gobbled it up. "Don't mind my sister," he told his fish. "She's weird."

Bobby picked up Wandee and stabbed the air with it like a sword. Then he noticed something odd. Rover was transfixed by the sparkly wand. When Bobby moved Wandee to the left, Rover moved to the left. When Bobby moved Wandee to the right, Rover moved to the right. When Wandee went up, so did Rover. When Wandee went down, Rover did too. It was as if Wandee were magical.

Bobby jumped up and down to make sure he wasn't dreaming. He walked around the room and came back to Rover's tank. Then Bobby waved Wandee slowly back and forth. His fish swam alongside it each time.

Bobby glanced at Mr. Huggums to see if he saw it too.

Rover could do tricks?

For the next week, Rover and Bobby worked on developing his tricks. At first Rover only followed Wandee, but
eventually Bobby began training him to respond to hand
signals. When he made a circle with his finger, Rover could
almost do an underwater flip. Bobby was especially pleased
when the fish started learning how to push a little plastic soccer ball. A couple of times he almost called Holly to tell her,
then stopped himself when he remembered that they weren't
speaking.

One morning Annie pounded on his closed door. "Squirt,
get your skinny self down to breakfast!" she yelled.

Bobby ignored her. He was in the middle of his morning
talk with Rover. "You won't believe this, but yesterday Holly
was with Jillian Zarr, and when I walked past them, Jillian
Zarr whispered, 'Where are your curlers?'"

Rover stopped swimming.

"I know!" Bobby cried. "She is so mean. And Holly's the
one who told her about the curlers. I wonder what else she's
told her about me?" His eyes grew big when he thought of

all the secrets that Holly knew — like that when he was a toddler he bit the mall Santa. Or that he cried when he watched *Old Yeller*. Or that he had been chased by a cat, twice.

Bobby untangled Diver Dave from a piece of plant and tried to think of more pleasant things. "Hey, when I get home from school we'll start learning how to swim through a hoop," he told Rover. "We'll also work on your zigzagging. Your zig could use some more practice, but your zag is excellent."

Before leaving his room, Bobby slipped Wandee under his bed for safekeeping. "See you later!" he told Rover.

After a breakfast of lumpy homemade oatmeal, Bobby carried his mother's briefcase out to the car for her. Mrs. Ellis-Chan opened the door to the cream-colored Volvo. Her car was always clean and smelled nice, unlike Mr. Ellis-Chan's messy Mini-Max Hybrid with its weird musty odor.

"Bobby," his mother said as she pressed some money into his hand, "this is for the bake sale. If your father's cookies aren't selling, I want you to buy some."

Bobby nodded solemnly. "I will," he promised. He knew how important the cookies were to his dad. For weeks Mr. Ellis-Chan had been perfecting his recipe.

As Bobby watched the Volvo head down the street, his dad joined him in the driveway. Casey was on his shoulders, blowing kisses to the passing cars. Mr. Ellis-Chan handed Bobby a plain brown paper sack. Cautiously, he looked inside. There was a peanut butter sandwich, a green apple, a juice box, and a black lump.

"Thanks, Dad. You're the best!"

With Casey still on his shoulders, Mr. Ellis-Chan scooped up his son and gave him a bear hug. "Stop!" Bobby shouted as he laughed. "I'm going to be late for school."

"Say hi to Holly for me," Casey sang. "Holly! Holly! Holly!"

Bobby just nodded. How could he tell her that he hadn't spoken to Holly for almost a week?

★★★ CHAPTER 9 ★★★

Field Trip Fun

ap tap. Tap tap. Tap tap. The sound of Mrs. Carlson's heels was comforting, like raindrops against a window. *Tap tap. Tap tap. Tap, tap, tap.* Suddenly the noise stopped.

"Bobby, you have a wonderfully unique style."

Bobby was startled to find Mrs. Carlson peering over his shoulder. The assignment was to draw the number-one thing you'd like to see at Huntington Gardens the next day. Bobby had considered drawing the lily ponds or one of the topiaries, but ultimately decided on the Koloff tree. In the brochure Mrs. Carlson had passed around, it said that the tree was very rare.

"Everyone, look at Bobby's interpretation of the Koloff tree." Mrs. Carlson held up his paper so the whole class could see it. "As we discussed, it's the stickiest and smelliest tree in the world. Bobby has drawn it leaning to one side, as if it were lonely."

Bobby paused. He had no idea he had drawn a lonely tree. But Mrs. Carlson was right, it did seem sad. *It probably doesn't have any friends*, he mused. The poor Koloff tree.

Before class was dismissed, Mrs. Carlson reminded everyone, "Please bring a sack lunch for the field trip. And don't forget your 'Why Elections Are Important' essays are due at the end of the week."

After school, Bobby headed to the PTA bake sale. Casey was under the table giggling. She had just tied Jackson's shoelaces together and he had fallen over. "Jackson, get up off the ground and stop playing around," his mother chided him.

Jillian Zarr's mom was the president of the PTA. She stood behind the bake sale cash box eyeing Mr. Ellis-Chan, who was arranging and rearranging the baked goods. One time at the grocery store, Mr. Ellis-Chan had sent Annie to get eggs. When she headed back to the cart, he jumped out from behind a potato-chip display and did his trademarked Freezer growl. Only he didn't surprise Annie — he surprised Mrs. Zarr. She screamed and threw her eggs into the air, leaving a huge mess in Aisle #10. After that, whenever Mrs. Zarr saw Mr. Ellis-Chan, she flinched.

Bobby joined Chess in front of the baked-goods table. Chess wasn't moving. Bobby suspected he was overwhelmed by the choices. Mrs. Zarr's bracelets jangled as she recited, ". . . lemon tarts, marble pound cake, Rice Krispies Treats, oatmeal cookies, snickerdoodles . . ." She skipped over Mr. Ellis-Chan's burnt cookies.

After long consideration, Chess selected a vanilla cupcake. He wiped off the frosting before taking a bite. "My palate is very sensitive," he explained.

Holly and Jillian Zarr strode toward the boys. "Hi, Holly!"

shouted Casey. She was still under the table. "Holly! Holly! Look at my new wand."

"It's beautiful!" Holly whistled. Bobby had always admired how well Holly could whistle. "What happened to Wandee?"

Casey's smile turned upside down. "Wandee's gone. Poof!"

Bobby pretended to be interested in a blueberry muffin.

"Hi, Mom." Jillian Zarr waved. "Where are our brownies?"

"Sold out," Mrs. Zarr replied, clearly pleased to announce this. The two of them looked alike.

"These cookies might be worth a try," Mr. Ellis-Chan suggested to Holly. He offered up the burnt ones.

"Are they chocolate?" Holly looked hopeful. On Halloween Bobby used to trade his chocolate candies for her red licorice and JawBlasters.

"Well, er, no. They're peanut butter," Mr. Ellis-Chan mumbled as he put them back down. "They may be slightly burnt. That's why they're discounted." He tried not to look disappointed when Holly chose a bag of chocolate chip cookies instead.

Bobby had been admiring the Rice Krispies Treats. The squares of gooey marshmallowy goodness had tons of sprinkles on them. Nearby were star-shaped sugar cookies capped with green icing, piles of coconut macaroons, and oatmeal cookies stuffed with raisins. As Bobby reached for a Rice Krispies Treat, he remembered his promise to his mother.

"Um, I'll take these," he said, grabbing a bag of burnt cookies instead.

Mr. Ellis-Chan nudged Mrs. Zarr in the ribs. She shrieked, then covered her mouth with both hands. "Those are mine," he boasted. "Do you want to try one?" Hands still over her mouth, Mrs. Zarr shook her head. "Bobby," his father said, "go ahead and give one to Mrs. Zarr."

Bobby handed a cookie to Jillian Zarr's mother. Reluctantly, she took a nibble, and when she thought no one was looking, she spit it out in a napkin.

Mr. Ellis-Chan pretended not to see this, and Bobby pretended not to see the hurt look on his father's face.

"These are so different!" Bobby said loudly, dipping into his bag of cookies. Somehow he managed to smile as he chewed. Even though Bobby's mouth felt like it had filled up with burnt cardboard, it was worth it to see his father grin.

The next morning Bobby got up early and bade Rover good-bye. He rushed through breakfast and tried to choke down the muffin his father baked. It had a strange mint flavor, like toothpaste. To wash away the taste, Bobby downed three glasses of milk. He slipped the rest of the muffin in his pants pocket so his dad would think he ate the whole thing.

Everyone from Room 15 was excited as they gripped their sack lunches and lined up on the sidewalk. The bus ride could be almost as much fun as the field trip itself. The boys scrambled to claim their seats. They all knew that if you weren't fast enough, you could end up next to a girl, and then the whole day would be ruined. But, if you were superfast, you got to sit by a friend and be next to the window. Then you could make faces at the cars down below.

Bobby didn't get a window seat. Still, he managed to grab a place next to Jackson, so at least he didn't have to sit next to a girl and risk getting cooties. As the bus roared past the Rialto Theater, Mrs. Carlson had everyone sing "The Wheels on the Bus Go Round and Round," first slow, then faster and faster, until no one could understand the words.

By the time they arrived at Huntington Gardens, the class was all revved up. Mrs. Carlson quickly divided the students into tour groups. Bobby's good news was that he was with Chess and St. James. His bad news was that Holly and Jillian Zarr were in the group as well — and Mrs. Zarr was their parent volunteer. Jillian Zarr and her mother were wearing matching green dresses and pointed shoes that looked like weapons. At least Holly had the good sense to wear sneakers and jeans.

The first stop for Bobby's group was the Desert Garden.

"Wow, these cactuses are so cool!" St. James shouted as he pretended to be a cowboy riding an invisible horse.

"It's *cacti*," Jillian Zarr corrected him. "That's the plural for *cactus*."

St. James held his nose. "What's plural for 'you stink'?"

"Look!" cried Holly. "A pachypodium lamerei!"

"It looks like a palm tree to me." St. James snorted.

"Read the sign." Holly sounded exasperated. She took a photo of the tree with her disposable camera. "It's also known as a Madagascar Palm."

Suddenly Chess started leaping up and down. "OUCH! Ouch, ouch, OUCH, ouch, ouch!"

"Did you touch a cacti?" Jillian Zarr said accusingly. "I'll bet you touched a cacti. Mommmmm, Chess touched a cacti!"

"It touched me," Chess howled as he examined his bleeding finger. "I'm dying! Call an ambulance! Ouch."

Mrs. Zarr frantically dug through her purse as the girls glared at Chess. Bobby noted that girls had two basic looks: angry and disgusted. When they yelled at you with their hands on their hips, it meant they were both. Chess had to suffer through wearing a Hello Little Ballerina Bear bandage on his finger. Still, it stopped the bleeding.

Holly consulted a map. "The Japanese Garden is this way," she said, pointing. "Follow me and try not to get into any trouble." She looked at Chess when she said this.

The lily pond looked like a mirror reflecting the white clouds and blue sky. Floating on the top of the water were pads of green leaves and bright fuchsia flowers. Giant koi glided silently just below the surface of the pond. "Some of the fish are over a hundred years old," Holly said, reading the sign. She snapped another photo.

St. James tossed a rock into the water. Ripples made their way to the banks as the koi scattered.

"Hey, stop that," Holly ordered.

"Who's going to make me?" St. James picked up another rock and held it over his head. Mrs. Zarr was far off in the distance.

"We are!" Jillian Zarr joined Holly.

St. James pretended to quiver. "Ooooh, I'm sooooo scared. Tell them, Bobby. Tell them we can do whatever we want!"

"Um, St. James," Bobby said apologetically, "Holly's right. You really shouldn't do that."

For a split second St. James looked wounded. "Whose side are you on?" he demanded. His face turned red as he stabbed the dirt with the heel of his shoe. St. James threw the rock into the bushes and stormed off.

As the group made its way toward the Jungle Garden, Bobby caught up with him to explain. "Sorry about that, but I have a pet fish, Rover. It's just that I wouldn't want anyone throwing a rock at him. I mean, that would really upset him. Or he could get hurt."

Jillian Zarr butted into the conversation. "Goldfish are stupid."

Bobby stood up straight. "Rover may look like an average fish, but once you get to know him, he's special. He can follow commands and do tricks, plus he's a great listener!"

"Like I'd have anything to say to a fish!" Jillian Zarr scoffed.

St. James threw a handful of leaves in her direction as she strutted away. He turned toward Bobby. "We have a tabby cat named Tabitha. But she doesn't do anything but hide and come out to eat."

"Rover can do a complete underwater flip and his zigzag is amazing," Bobby boasted. He watched Jillian Zarr whispering to Holly.

Chess joined the boys and nodded. "You should see Rover zigging and zagging. Hey, let's act like Rover and zigzag to the Jungle Garden!"

"Race you there," St. James shouted.

As they took off, they could hear Mrs. Zarr calling, "Boys! Boys, please, we're supposed to stick together!"

The boys ran in different directions, met up, and split up again, laughing the whole time. Bobby felt like he was flying. He put his arms out to his sides so he would be more aerodynamic. What could be more fun than this?

Bobby loved field trips.

CHAPTER 10

The Rare Koloff Tree

Bobby hated field trips. Where did everyone go?

The Jungle Garden was huge. Weird shrubs and sinister vines were everywhere. Bobby hoped there weren't any cheetahs or apes nearby. Annie had once forced him to watch a scary movie featuring apes who had taken over the earth. It didn't end well.

Bobby soon realized that if he was going to be rescued, he needed to be found first. That's when he had a brilliant idea. He reached into his pocket and pulled out the minty muffin. Like Hansel and Gretel, he could leave a trail of crumbs behind him!

When the muffin was gone, Bobby searched his pockets again, but this time he pulled out only bits of lint. As he dropped them on the ground, he noticed that the plants were so dense and the trees were so tall they blocked the sunlight.

Bobby began to panic. Maybe no one would find the bits of minty muffin, the scraps of lint, or him — ever.

At last, Bobby stumbled into a clearing. Something smelled bad. Really bad. Like really, really, really bad. Bobby looked around to see if someone had farted. He had never smelled anything that bad before. It was worse than the old lady with the blue hair at church who wore way too much perfume.

Just as he was about to turn on his heels and flee, he saw IT.

The Koloff tree was much smaller than Bobby had imagined. The trunk was yellow-greenish, with layers of peeling bark. Beautiful white flowers bloomed all over its branches. However, according to Mrs. Carlson, the flowers were what produced its horrible smell — and that, Bobby realized, was what he was smelling at that very moment.

Like Bobby's drawing, the tree looked sad. It probably didn't get many visitors. There weren't any plants close by. Even the birds kept their distance. But Bobby was drawn toward the tree. He held his breath as he studied its flowers. Their petals were in full bloom and looked incredibly thick and sturdy, yet soft at the same time. In the center of each flower was a small bulb that resembled an orange JawBlaster candy cracked open. Despite the smell, the Koloff tree was really wondrous, like something out of *Princess Becky's Planet*.

If only people could get past the stink, Bobby thought, *then they'd know what a special tree this is.*

Without thinking, he opened his arms and gave the Koloff tree a huge hug. "Don't worry, stinky tree," he whispered. "I'll be your friend."

After a moment, Bobby stiffened. The tree smelled even worse up close, but when he attempted to step back, his arms remained tight around the trunk. The harder he tried to get away, the more stuck he got. The sticky stuff was all over his shirt. It was on his arms. The foul smell was making him ill. Scary thoughts began to bubble in Bobby's brain.

What if no one ever finds me?

What if I am stuck here forever?

What if I have to go to the bathroom?

Why did I drink so much milk at breakfast?

"Help! Someone help me!" he cried.

★ ★ ★

The time dragged by. Bobby tried to pull free occasionally, but the tree's sap had started to harden, holding him even more firmly. This was a million times worse than the static cling that made socks and other clothing stick to the Ellis-Chan family.

As the day wore on, Bobby started to get used to the stink. He wished he could sit down, but of course that was impossible. To pass the time, he told the Koloff tree about his family and his grandparents and Rover. Just as Bobby was recounting the time his dad accidentally left him behind at Pizza Palace, he heard someone yell, "Robert Carver Ellis-Chan, leave that tree alone!"

What?!?!

Holly stood at the entrance to the clearing. Jillian Zarr and her mother were right behind her. They all had their hands on their hips.

"Bobby, please step away from the tree," Mrs. Zarr said. He could tell from the pinched look on her face that she was trying not to act upset.

"I can't," he said weakly.

"Stop kidding around," Holly ordered. She snapped a photo of Bobby hugging the tree.

"I can't let go." Bobby raised his voice. "I'm stuck!"

Chess and St. James appeared behind the girls. St. James was dragging a huge dried-up palm leaf.

"Hey, what are you doing?" Chess asked. He pointed a big stick at Bobby. "You're not hugging that tree, are you?"

Jillian Zarr held her nose. "He claims he's stuck."

Chess circled the Koloff tree, examining Bobby from every angle. "He really is stuck," he reported. "Oh, wow, it stinks! Holly, did you fart?"

Holly glared at Chess with such force that he jumped backward.

"Oh dear," Mrs. Zarr murmured as she held a tissue over her nose. "Oh dear, oh my. Oh dear, oh my."

Everyone was holding their noses but Bobby. He was holding a tree.

St. James suggested, "How about we pull him off?" He and Chess came close and yanked on the back of Bobby's shirt. But Bobby didn't budge and neither did the Koloff tree.

"This is not good." Mrs. Zarr's voice was getting higher. "Not good at all."

"Wait, I've got it!" Chess lit up. "Let's dig up the tree and Bobby can just take it with him."

Bobby imagined himself and the Koloff tree playing with Rover.

Bobby imagined himself and the Koloff tree skateboarding.

Bobby imagined himself and the Koloff tree trick-or-treating.

He let out a loud pitiful groan.

"Maybe," Jillian Zarr interrupted, "we ought to just leave him here."

"That sounds like an excellent idea," Holly agreed.

"You boys stay with Bobby," Mrs. Zarr said. She was positively squeaking. "Girls, you come with me. We're going for help."

When Mrs. Carlson entered the clearing and saw Bobby hugging the Koloff tree, she came to a dead halt. Her mouth hung open and she held her nose. So did the entire population of Room 15 and all the parent volunteers. It was like they were playing Simon Says and Mrs. Carlson was the leader.

Finally, Bobby broke the silence. "It was an accident."

Mrs. Carlson began to cry. Bobby's throat tightened. Sure, people cried all the time at school. There wasn't a recess when someone wasn't crying. But a teacher crying was unheard of. Did it mean he'd be stuck to a tree forever?

Then he heard a familiar sound — a snort. Mrs. Carlson wasn't crying; she was laughing! Soon everyone in the clearing was doubled over in hysterics. Bobby shut his eyes.

"Well, this really isn't funny. It's very serious," Mrs. Carlson said as she wiped away her tears. "Are you all right, Bobby? I'm so sorry I laughed, it's just that . . . well, this is not the sort of thing I see every day."

Before he could respond, Mrs. Zarr came running back. She was still panting as she began to babble to Mrs. Carlson. "He ran away — couldn't stop him — boy is dangerous — his father too!"

As Mrs. Carlson attempted to calm Mrs. Zarr down, a sturdy woman wearing a green shirt and brown pants approached. She didn't act surprised to see him stuck to a tree. "Bobby, I'm Lacy. I'm a naturalist here. Are you okay? How do you feel?"

"Fine," he fibbed.

On Mrs. Carlson's orders, Mrs. Zarr and the other parent volunteers herded the kids away. Mrs. Carlson stayed behind. Lacy started taking bottles out of her knapsack. "Bobby, this will unstick you, all right?"

His stomach filled with worry. What was it? Some sort of poison? As if reading his mind, Lacy reassured him, "It's just shampoo." She tucked her long red hair under her hat. "I'm going to pour it on you and then we'll slide you off. This won't hurt you or the tree." She opened a couple of the bottles. "By the way, how did you get stuck?"

"There was a snake chasing me, and I was running so fast I didn't see the tree," Bobby said in a rush. "I couldn't stop because I had picked up so much speed, and then, SMACK! I was stuck."

Lacy smiled gently. "Bobby, were you hugging the tree?"

"Yes," he admitted. His cheeks burned.

Lacy laughed as she began pouring shampoo over him. It was slippery and warm. "I thought so. The Koloff tree gets about one hugger a month."

"Really?"

"Really. Usually there's a fence around it, but it's being

repaired. Want to know a secret?" Bobby nodded. "I got stuck to the Koloff tree too," Lacy confessed.

For the first time since being stuck, Bobby was able to smile.

On the bus ride back to school, not only did Bobby get a window seat, he had five rows all to himself.

The first thing Bobby did when he got home was run upstairs and tell Rover, "You won't believe what happened!"

Casey poked her head into the room. "Daddy says to hurry up and take a bath. Here, Bobby," she said, handing him something.

He looked down, surprised. "But this is yours."

Casey nodded. "Yes, but you need it more than me."

Bobby took the Princess Becky bubble bath. "Thanks, Casey."

His little sister smiled sweetly. "You're welcome, Bobby. But I have to go now. You smell like poop."

★★★ CHAPTER 11 ★★★

N-o-m-i-n-a-t-i-o-n-s

For the next few days Jillian Zarr and her wolf pack held their noses whenever they saw Bobby. A couple of fifth-grade boys called him a "tree hugger," but Bobby shrugged it off. "There are worse things you can call a person," he explained to Rover one evening. "Besides, when I left, I think the Koloff tree stood a little straighter."

Soon enough the drama of Bobby being stuck to a tree blew over and was replaced with new excitement. "We will be voting for our student council representative next week," Mrs. Carlson told the class as she collected their election essays. Bobby had worked very hard on his and had even drawn an American flag on the front page — only he had added too many stars and had to cross some out. "And that means that today we will have nominations."

Bobby glanced up from his notebook. He had been

doodling a picture of Rover playing with his ball. No one knew about Rover's supersecret soccer-playing abilities — yet. Bobby planned to put on a big show for his family and debut Rover's amazing talents. Maybe he'd even make posters and serve popcorn, Bobby mused. Rover was doing so well, he'd be ready in about a week or so. He didn't even need Wandee that much anymore.

Mrs. Carlson brought Bobby out of his daydream. "Right, Bobby?"

"Huh?"

"The student council is very important," she repeated.

"Um, yes. Right," he said, nodding vigorously to make up for not paying attention.

"Good," his teacher said. "After recess we'll have nominations. So be thinking of who you'd like to represent Room 15 at student council meetings."

As the boys waited their turns on the handball court, Chess said, "I would run, but chess club takes up all of my time."

Chess had recently started the club and appointed himself president. So far the only members were him and an intense fifth-grade girl who didn't like to lose. Chess had been trying to recruit Bobby, first by begging, then with threats. "If you don't join and it's just me and that girl, I may throw up every day, and it would be all your fault."

Still, Bobby refused. He didn't want Chess to know that he always got the bishop and the rook mixed up. Or was it the castle and the knight? The only thing he knew for sure was that the short ones were the prawns.

"What about you?" St. James asked as he tossed the handball to Bobby.

"What about me?" Bobby hit the ball as hard as he could. Handball didn't make him nearly as nervous as other sports like soccer or baseball, where, if you messed up, people got mad at you.

"You should run for student council," St. James said as he returned the serve with a slam so hard that Bobby ducked.

Bobby scrambled to hit it back. "Why me?"

Whomp! St. James returned the ball. "'Cause everyone likes you."

The handball hit Bobby in the shoulder and bounced away, but he hardly noticed. He was too busy thinking about what St. James just said.

Bobby went to the end of the line.

"Yeah, Bobby," Jackson jumped in. "You should definitely

run for student council rep. You're not the best at anything, but not the worst. So no one's threatened by you. You're just there."

"Uh, thanks, I guess," Bobby said. He imagined his campaign slogan: *Bobby. He's just there.*

"You've gotta run," St. James insisted as he waited his turn to play again. "Otherwise some girl might be our class rep, and we can't have that!"

"NO GIRLS!" the boys yelled.

"Girls stink!" St. James shouted and kicked his foot into the air.

"Bobby stinks!" Jillian Zarr yelled back from near the tetherball poles. She held her nose.

As St. James and Jillian Zarr continued to fling insults at each other, Bobby considered running for rep. It would be cool to be elected. Plus everyone knew that there were unlimited free donuts at student council meetings. He wondered if they had the glazed buttermilk kind. Glazed was good, but glazed buttermilks were the best.

After recess, his heart beat a little faster when Mrs. Carlson wrote N-o-m-i-n-a-t-i-o-n-s on the board. "Okay, class, who would like to go first?"

Everyone looked around expectantly. Finally, St. James stood and placed his hand over his heart. "I, St. James Odysseus Plunkett, would hereby and so forth and lawfully and here-with upon my constitution pledge on my honor —"

"St. James," Mrs. Carlson cut in, "is there someone you would like to nominate?"

"Him!" St. James pointed. "Bobby Ellis-Chan!"

Bobby felt the heat of everyone staring at him.

"Bobby," said Mrs. Carlson, "do you accept St. James's nomination?"

He nodded.

Mrs. Carlson wrote B-O-B-B-Y on the board. It looked good up there. Bobby imagined himself winning. Maybe he'd have business cards like his mom.

"Who else would like to nominate someone?" Mrs. Carlson asked. When no one spoke up, she said, "All right, then. If there

are no other nominees, Bobby will run unopposed and automatically become Room 15's student council representative!"

Bobby squeezed his eyes shut and imagined himself holding a plate piled high with glazed buttermilk donuts. Just as he was about to take a bite, someone shouted, "I nominate Holly Harper!"

Instantly, the donuts disappeared. Bobby opened his eyes to see Mrs. Carlson reaching for her marker. "Holly, do you accept Jillian's nomination?"

"I accept," Holly announced loudly and clearly.

The girls cheered.

"Any other nominations? This is the last call." Mrs. Carlson looked around the room. "Okay! It's official. Bobby and Holly are our candidates. You each have one week to campaign. The elections will take place next Tuesday."

"I'm voting for Holly," a girl said.

"Bobby has my vote," a boy promised.

Everyone in the class was talking all at once. Everyone but Bobby and Holly. They just glanced at each other, then turned away.

CHAPTER 12

Boys vs. Girls

"Well, what are we going to do?" Chess asked.

"About what?" Bobby slid over to make room for him at the lunch table.

"As your campaign manager, I'm telling you we need a plan." As usual, Chess was having a cheese sandwich on Wonder Bread. He had eaten the same thing for lunch every day since kindergarten. The only time it changed was when his grandmother visited from India. Then he'd eat his cheese sandwich on chapati bread.

"How about we all vote for him?" St. James said through a mouthful of food, so it sounded like, "Wow bout woe wall wote for im?"

"Of course we're going to vote for him," Chess assured him. "But we have to make sure the rest of Room 15 votes for Bobby too."

Just then Jillian Zarr marched over. No girls were allowed at the boys' table. It just wasn't done. But that didn't stop her from standing over them all with a cross look on her face. She was wearing blue nail polish that matched the ridiculous bows in her pigtails. Bobby felt sure that she was the one who made Holly wear nail polish. Jillian Zarr was a bad influence.

"I just wanted to tell you worms that Bobby doesn't have a chance," Jillian Zarr said smugly.

Chess stood on the bench to confront her. "I'm Bobby's campaign manager," he said loudly. "And I say you're wrong."

"Well, you're looking at Holly's campaign manager," Jillian Zarr replied with a smirk. "And I'm never wrong. Let's face it, boys, you'd better get used to losing. Girls rule!"

This was enough to make St. James gag on his hamburger. "BOOF ROOF!!!" he yelled. When Jillian Zarr looked at him blankly, he swallowed his food, then repeated more clearly, "BOYS RULE! It's boys versus girls and the boys will win!!!"

"Urgggg!!!!" Jillian Zarr shook her head and retreated.

"Are you okay, Bobby?" Chess asked as he sat back down. "You look like you just ate a slug."

"I'm fine," he said, even though he wasn't. What if Jillian Zarr was right and he didn't have a chance? What if he lost big-time to Holly?

As St. James hurled insults at the girls, Chess chewed his sandwich and studied Bobby like he was a science experiment. Finally Chess announced, "We need to do this campaign like professionals. We'll need posters."

"And bumper stickers," St. James added.

"Television commercials!" Jackson jumped in.

"Buttons!"

"A campaign bus!"

"An airplane!"

Chess asked, "How much money do you have, Bobby?"

"Twelve dollars," he answered, then remembered maybe it was eleven since he just bought a new yo-yo string. "But I'm saving up for new toys for Rover."

"We'll have to go low-budget then," Chess conceded.

"Well," St. James began. He stopped to take the straw out of his juice box and squeeze the rest of the Orange Guzzle into his mouth. "At least we can have a really great poster. Bobby, you're good at drawing."

Bobby blushed. He had been working hard on his drawings. Lately he had replaced most of his dog pictures with portraits of Rover. One was so good that his mom even bought a fancy gold frame for it and hung it in the living room.

"Okay, then," Chess said. "Bobby will make an awesome poster and come up with freebies to hand out. And we'll talk him up to all the boys and get their vote."

Bobby nodded. It sounded like a good plan. He couldn't help but grin as the boys chanted, "Go, Bobby, go! Go, Bobby, go! Go, Bobby, go!"

The more he thought about his nomination, the more excited Bobby became. "Mrs. Carlson said this is a very important job," he told Rover that night. "You represent the entire class at student council meetings. That's where they discuss major stuff like recess and the lunch menu."

Rover did a loop around the aquarium to show his support. Soon the two started working on the soccer ball trick. Rover was getting quite good at pushing the ball with his

nose. Several times he almost made it into the net that Bobby had fashioned out of chopsticks and a piece of cloth.

Casey strolled in wearing a new crown. Quickly, Bobby pulled Wandee out of the water and tossed it across the room, out of sight.

"Hi, Fishy-fish-fish!" Casey cooed as she peered at Rover. "Bobby, make him twirl."

Using hand signals, Bobby gave Rover the command. As he did a backflip, Casey clapped. She was wearing her Princess Becky pajamas and had just taken her bubble bath, so she smelled like flowers. "Does Fishy-fish-fish ever take a bath?"

"His name's Rover. And he doesn't need to take a bath, he's a fish," Bobby explained for the hundredth time. He wiped her fingerprints off the aquarium glass.

"Fish don't get dirty?" Casey asked. She pressed her nose up against the tank.

"Nope."

Casey squinted at Rover. "But he swims in his pee," she pointed out.

"That's why I have to clean the aquarium."

"I think it's bad that Fishy-fish-fish has to swim in pee," she insisted. "It's mean! Poor fish! You're mean, Bobby!" Suddenly Casey screamed. "Bobby! There's string coming out of Rover's behind!"

Bobby took his math homework out of his backpack. "That's not string," he said matter-of-factly. "Rover's pooping."

Casey's mouth hung open in disbelief. "He pees *and* poops in the water?"

"That's what fish do," Bobby started to explain. Before he could say anything more, Casey made a choking noise, then ran out of the room shrieking.

"It's okay," Bobby assured Rover. "You're just being yourself. There's nothing wrong with that." He sat down at his desk and took out his colored pencils. "You know, the one weird part of this election is that I'm running against Holly.

You met her. She's the one who gave you to me. Of course, that's when we used to be sorta-best friends, only these days she's my enemy." He paused. It felt weird to call Holly his enemy. "We used to do everything together. And now she's running against me on purpose! St. James says it's a war. Boys versus girls. But it's really me against Holly Harper."

The more he told Rover about Holly, the angrier he got. He shoved his math homework aside and pulled out the poster board his mom had brought home. Bobby drew a picture of Holly with her hair before it had been Jillian Zarr-icized and straightened. He dotted her face with a marker to make her freckles, and instead of her usual smile, he drew a squiggly line. Bobby then added horns on her head and a fancy mustache under her nose. When Rover saw it, he did a backflip.

"I know," Bobby laughed. "Pretty funny! I should take this to school, except that Jillian Zarr and the wolf pack would probably rip it apart."

Bobby started thinking about his real campaign poster. On a new board in big bold letters he wrote, "Vote For Bobby for Student consil rep."

The word *council* didn't look right, plus the letters were way too small. He turned the poster board over. "Vote for

Bobby for Student Concil Rep!!!" This time the letters were too big at the beginning and squashed at the end. Bobby used the back of the Holly picture and slowly wrote, "Vote for Bobby for Studint Council."

Satisfied, he considered what to draw. Mrs. Carlson had said that a great campaign had a memorable slogan. She told the class that former President Jimmy Carter, who was once a peanut farmer, campaigned on a promise of "Not Just Peanuts," and Dwight Eisenhower used his nickname in "I like Ike." Bobby didn't even have a nickname, unless you counted when Annie called him Squirt. But "Squirt for Student Council" didn't sound very good.

Bobby watched Rover skimming the bottom of his aquarium, just above the rocks. Then it hit him! "Rover, you're a genius," he cried.

With great enthusiasm, Bobby drew a mountain of rocks with himself standing on top of it. Then he added the words *Bobby Rocks!*

"Now everyone's sure to know who I am," Bobby announced.

Rover zigzagged his approval.

★★★ CHAPTER 13 ★★★

Poster Problems

Bobby left his skateboard on the front porch, next to Casey's purple and pink Princess Big Wheel. He couldn't very well skate to school and carry his excellent campaign poster. Plus, his pockets were filled with rocks, making it hard for him to balance.

As Bobby made his way down the street, he had to keep stopping to pull his pants up. The rocks were weighing them down. When he neared the house with the scary cat, Bobby quickened his pace. The cat was staring at him with its tail pointed straight up. It had twenty-seven toes, maybe more. Neither Bobby nor Holly had ever been brave enough to count.

Mr. Kirby was waiting at the corner. Bobby put down his poster, pulled up his pants, and then steadied the crossing guard as he rose from his lawn chair. Mr. Kirby brought the

poster up to his nose to examine it. "Are you in a rock band?" he asked.

"No," Bobby explained. "*Bobby Rocks!* means that, you know, I'm sort of cool." As proof, he gave Mr. Kirby a rock. "See you after school!"

Mr. Kirby was still staring at the rock as Bobby headed toward the playground.

Chess jumped off the monkey bars when he saw Bobby. "I'll put up the poster," he offered. "Mrs. Carlson's room is unlocked. Did you bring your campaign freebies?" Bobby nodded and tugged at his pants. "Well, get going," Chess urged him. "Holly's almost already done passing out her campaign material. Look!" He handed Bobby a bookmark that read, BE SMART. VOTE FOR HOLLY. It looked professional, plus there was a lollipop taped to it.

Jillian Zarr was following Holly around. So were some other girls from the wolf pack. "Vote for Holly," they told everyone in Mrs. Carlson's class.

Bobby gave rocks to all the boys in Room 15. A few even asked for two. But when he approached a group of girls, none of them would take one. Some even held their noses. St. James, Jackson, and Chess shook their heads in disgust as they sucked on their lollipops. "Do they have to do everything together?" Chess asked. "They're so infuriating."

The bell rang. All over the playground, students scattered, then lined up in front of their classrooms. Mrs. Carlson strolled up to Room 15 and opened the door. When Bobby stepped into the classroom, he was stunned by Holly's poster. It looked dazzling. A ton of red, white, and blue glitter surrounded a photo of her reading a book titled *Democracy for All*. However, right next to Holly's poster was something even more shocking.

Jillian Zarr whipped around and pointed accusingly at Bobby. "That is so NOT funny!"

In a panic, Bobby turned to Chess. "Why is that there?"

Chess threw his arms up in the air. "Because you gave it to me?"

"But that's the wrong side!" Bobby moaned. He covered his face with his hands. Even though he had drawn horns and a mustache, you could still tell the girl was Holly. The boys were cracking up, but all the girls looked like they had sucked on lemons.

"Class!" Mrs. Carlson turned the lights on and off. "Please calm down. Chess, remove the poster. Bobby, I'd like to see you outside."

Bobby's stomach sank. After "I'm going to have to call your parents," "I'd like to see you outside" was the worst thing a teacher could say.

Even though he'd given away half his rocks, his body felt heavy. Bobby dragged himself toward the door and prepared for his doom.

★ ★ ★

Mrs. Carlson was frowning. She'd never frowned at Bobby before. Mostly she smiled. Bobby wished he was with Rover. In his room. In bed. With the lights out. Under the covers. And it was the weekend. And he was old, like thirty-one years old, and this was over.

"Bobby?" Mrs. Carlson said.

"I didn't mean for anyone to see that," he stammered. "I ran out of poster board. The other side has my student council poster on it. I promise! You can look at it." He felt his throat tighten. "I'm sorry."

Mrs. Carlson gave Bobby a weary smile. "Bobby, get up off your knees. It's not me you should be apologizing to."

Bobby slouched to the front of the room with his hands in his pockets. He wrapped his fingers around a rock to help calm himself down. "Holly . . ." His voice sounded scratchy. He cleared his throat and started over. "Holly, I'm sorry about the picture. . . ."

"I put up the wrong side," Chess interrupted. "It's all my fault. Sue me!"

Holly ignored him. She was too busy trying to bore holes through Bobby with her eyes.

"It was a mistake!" Bobby insisted. His words tumbled over each other. "I was just doodling and . . . whatever. No one was supposed to see that. I'm sorry."

Jillian Zarr raised her hand. "Mrs. Carlson, does this mean that Bobby is disqualified from running for student council rep? Because I think he should be."

Several girls nodded. They looked like bobblehead dolls.

"I don't know," Mrs. Carlson replied. "Holly, what do you think? Should Bobby be allowed to stay in the election?"

The longer Holly glared at Bobby, the more he squirmed. Finally she spoke. "In a democracy, everyone has the right to freedom of speech. Just because Bobby did something dumb, not to mention rude, it doesn't mean he shouldn't be able to run for student council."

"Well, Bobby?" Mrs. Carlson said. "Holly says you should still be able to run. Are you in the race?"

Bobby looked at the girls in the room shaking their heads and the boys nodding. Chess gave him a thumbs-up. "I'm still in, I guess," Bobby said weakly.

At lunch, Bobby was mobbed by the boys from his class. "I didn't do it on purpose!" he insisted.

"Oh, right, like I believe you," Jackson crowed, slapping Bobby on the back. "That Holly poster is classic. You really showed those girls!"

Bobby looked at the crush of jubilant boys. *This is what it's like to be popular*, he noted. But something about it didn't feel quite right. Bobby broke away and headed toward the swings, where Holly and the wolf pack were gathered.

"Um, Holly, can I talk to you?"

"Don't go," Jillian Zarr snapped as she and the other girls stood with their hands on their hips.

"Please, Holly," Bobby begged. "It won't take long."

"Oh, I suppose." Holly still sounded mad. A couple of years ago all he had to do was stick a crayon in his nose and Holly would crack up and forget why she was angry. Bobby wished he had a crayon in his pocket now.

The two walked toward the drinking fountain. The wolf pack followed them closely, ready to pounce at any moment.

"Holly, I'm sorry. Really."

"I know," she said, letting go of a long sigh.

"You do?"

"Yeah. And I hope you know that I had no idea Jillian would tell everyone that you were wearing pink curlers."

"Then I guess we're even," he said. Bobby's heart beat faster when he spied a hint of a smile on Holly's face.

"It was actually a pretty good picture of me," she admitted. "Except for the horns and the mustache."

Both broke out laughing. Relief washed over Bobby. For a brief moment, it felt like old times. Then Jillian Zarr stomped her foot. "Come on, Holly," she called out. "Stop talking to that stinkpot!"

Holly shrugged. "Bobby, I gotta go."

"Yeah, me too. Hey, Holly —" Bobby stopped and took a breath. "Thanks for letting me stay in the election. You didn't have to do that."

"I know," she said. "Good luck, Bobby."

"Good luck, Holly."

★★★ CHAPTER 14 ★★★

The Funeral Suit

The election was one day away, and Bobby still hadn't written his speech. He had started it several times but never got past "Hello, my name is Bobby." What was he supposed to say? He kept thinking about Holly. She was never at a loss for words. He wished they were still friends instead of opponents so she could help him with his speech.

Bobby's mind wandered back to the Koloff tree. The Koloff tree didn't have anyone on its side either. None of the other plants or birds would even get near it. It stood alone. Suddenly, Bobby was inspired to write.

Dear Mr. Koloff Tree,
It was nice meeting you. I hope you are well.
I enjoyed the time we spent together. I am sorry that

you had to get shampoo poured all over you. Even though you have a unique smell, I still think you are the best tree I have ever met.

Best wishes, your friend,
Bobby Ellis-Chan (the boy who hugged you)

P.S. I am running for Room 15 student council rep. If I ever had to vote for best tree, I'd vote for you.

In the margin, Bobby drew a picture of himself and the Koloff tree. Both stood tall.

Next he wrote a thank-you letter to Lacy at Huntington Gardens and added eleven dollars so she could buy more shampoo. He tucked in the letter to the Koloff tree as well. As Bobby sealed the envelope, he heard three fast knocks on the door, followed by a low whistle, then a lion's roar. "Come in, Chess!" Bobby called out.

Chess had a big garment bag slung over his shoulder. He handed it to Bobby, then bent down to say hello to Rover, who was practicing swimming through a hoop. Bobby unzipped the bag. "What's this for?" he asked, holding up a navy blue suit.

"I had to wear it to my great-uncle Checkers's funeral," Chess explained. "I barely even knew the guy, but my mother made me go. Have you ever been to a funeral?"

"No."

"Well, you're lucky. It's a bunch of people blowing their noses and crying. Here, try it on."

"Chess, no way!"

"As your campaign manager, I say you will. You want to win, right?"

Bobby nodded. He did want to win. It surprised him how much winning meant to him.

"Then you have to look good," Chess said. "You have to look sincere and smart and serious. Oh, and make sure you don't have any boogers hanging out. Something like that could ruin your chances of winning. Try it on — it'll make you look distinguished."

While Rover showed off his backflips and zigzags, Bobby put on the suit. "The sleeves are so long, I can't even see my hands," he complained.

"My mom got me a big size so I can grow into it," Chess explained without taking his eyes off of Rover. "I guess she thinks there will be lots of funerals in my future. C'mon. Let's hear your speech."

"Um . . . I was just working on it now. What should I say?"

Chess flopped on the bed. "Gee, Bobby, do I have to do everything for you? Writing is easy. Tell me why you want to be rep."

Bobby gave it some serious thought. "For the donuts?"

"No, you can't say that. What else?"

"Because I can't let the guys down?"

Chess sat up. "You've got something there. Do you have some index cards?" Bobby nodded. "Okay, write down the thing about the guys on there. Now write down that you would be proud to be rep 'cause you've got a lot of good ideas."

"But I don't," Bobby protested.

"Write it down," Chess ordered. After dictating a few more suggestions, he said, "Okay, now read your speech to me."

Bobby picked up his index cards. "Fine voters of Room 15 —"

"STOP!" Chess shouted. "Slow down. Lower your voice. Look sincere."

"Fine voters —" Bobby began again.

"STOP!" Chess barked. "Stand up straight. Speak up. Smile. Look sincere."

"Chess! Do you want me to look sincere or to smile?"

"Yes! And try not to look like you've just seen a ghost."

After Bobby gave his speech five times, Chess stretched out his arms and yawned. "Bobby, don't take this the wrong way, but it's really dull and boring. You could put the entire class to sleep. You could put the whole school to sleep. You could put the whole town to —"

"But it's what you told me to write," Bobby wailed. He slumped in his chair.

"You're the one who wrote it," Chess said defensively. "I just helped."

Both boys were silent, each deep in thought.

"I've got it!" Chess finally yelled. "If you have a really dynamic ending, no one will remember how boring the beginning was."

Bobby nodded. Chess had something there. It was like dessert. If you had chocolate cake for dessert, it made you forget about the Brussels sprouts. He thought about what might make a good ending. Princess Becky always ended her show with a song, but he wasn't about to sing in public. "How about this?" Bobby finally asked. "Knock knock.

"Who's there?

"Bobby.

"Bobby who?

"Bobby, your student council rep, that's who!" He grinned. "What do you think of that?"

But Chess didn't answer. He had fallen asleep on the bed.

That night Bobby tossed and turned and fought with his pillow. He dreamt that when he got to his dynamic ending, the entire class was snoring — including Mrs. Carlson. In the morning, he was so tangled up in his sheets that he had to yell for his mother to help him get out of bed.

As Bobby got dressed, the static from his T-shirt made his hair even more wild than usual. He slipped into the jacket of Chess's funeral suit. It practically swallowed him whole. Bobby felt ill. What was he doing? What was he thinking? He was just Bobby. How could he even imagine he'd win an election?

Bobby took Mr. Huggums down from the shelf and gave him a squeeze. Then he turned to Rover. "I'll see you after school, buddy. Wish me luck."

Rover circled the tank twice before pushing his soccer ball into the net. Astonished, Bobby shouted, "You did it! Rover, you did it!"

Rover always did know how to cheer him up.

"You look funny," Casey said as Bobby took his seat at the breakfast table.

"I think you look nice," Mrs. Ellis-Chan assured Bobby. She pulled a pair of Casey's pink ballet tights off of her dress. "Good luck with your speech and the election, Bobby."

"Remember to breathe," Annie told him as Mr. Ellis-Chan set a bowl of soupy oatmeal in front of her.

"If you get nervous," his father added, "just focus on one person in the audience."

"And if you get scared, shut your eyes and sing," Casey suggested. "Then Da-Da-Doo the dragon will come rescue you."

Bobby had a lot on his mind as he headed to school. To skateboard would have been dangerous. The pant legs on Chess's funeral suit were so long he kept tripping over himself.

Bobby slowed down when he spotted Holly leaving her house. He hid behind a tree and watched her kiss her mother good-bye. She was wearing a Girl Scout uniform covered with badges and pins. When did she become a Girl Scout? Bobby gulped and pushed his sleeves up. Holly looked impressive, like someone who was about to win an election.

CHAPTER 15

Election Day

"D on't you look nice," Mrs. Carlson commented as Bobby took his seat. He gave her a weak smile and wondered if it would be rude if he barfed.

Bobby glanced at Jillian Zarr. She was wearing a Girl Scout uniform too, and so were three other girls from their wolf pack. They looked united.

An election booth made out of a big cardboard box stood in the back of the room. "After each of you casts your vote," Mrs. Carlson told the class, "you will get a flag sticker."

St. James whispered loudly, "I'm going to vote twice to get two."

To Bobby's relief, Holly volunteered to deliver her speech first. This gave him more time to figure out how to disappear. Holly went up to the front of the room.

"If you're smart, you use a spoon, not a fork, when you eat ice cream," Holly said confidently. She wasn't even using notes! Bobby glanced at Jillian Zarr, who was quietly reciting Holly's speech along with her. He looked back at Holly in time to hear her say, ". . . so, if you're smart, you turn in your homework on time, and if you're smart, you vote for me, Holly Harper, for your Room 15 student council representative!"

The girls clapped and cheered while the boys looked bored.

Bobby was disappointed to find out he hadn't disappeared, although he did feel like he was shrinking in the oversized funeral suit.

"Don't forget your dynamic ending!" Chess whispered as Bobby dragged himself to the front of the room. The suit felt stiff. Bobby felt itchy. He tried to remember to stand up straight and to smile and to look sincere and to look serious.

"Bobby, are you all right?" Mrs. Carlson asked. She hurried over to him and put her hand on his forehead. Her hand felt cool. "Hmm . . . no fever."

"Um, I'm okay." He took a deep breath and dropped his index cards. Horrified, he scrambled to pick them up, but his pants were so long he tripped and fell. He looked up in time to see Chess slap himself in the forehead.

Bobby stood up and read his first index card. "Who's there?" he said. But that was from the knock-knock joke. . . . His notes were all out of order! Bobby began to sweat. He went ahead and finished the knock-knock joke, even though it was supposed to be his dynamic ending. It didn't matter anyway. No one laughed.

Bobby remembered his father's advice and tried to focus on one person in the room. But when he looked up, all he could see was Jillian Zarr smirking at him. So instead, he tried to focus on not passing out. His mouth felt like it was full of cotton, yet somehow he kept muddling forward. The class looked bored, and Bobby couldn't blame them. Even he was bored by his own speech.

"So, in conclusion . . ." Bobby mumbled. "That's it."

There was a smattering of applause, led by St. James. Bobby halfheartedly took a bow, as Chess had told him to do. He was sweating so much he felt like he was swimming. Bobby took off the suit jacket and shuffled back to his seat in silence.

Suddenly, one side of the room erupted in laughter. When Bobby turned around, the other side started howling. He turned around and around, trying to see if someone was doing something weird behind his back. The laughter only got louder.

What? What is it? Bobby wondered. Why wouldn't anyone let him in on the joke?

Bobby heard a familiar crackling sound as Jillian Zarr peeled something off his back. "Bobby, I believe this is yours," she said, waving a purple piece of material high in the air.

Slowly it dawned on him. *He* was the joke.

"Static cling," Bobby said weakly as he grabbed the purple thing from Jillian Zarr — Casey's Princess Becky underpants.

No one could hear him over the laughter. St. James was doubled over on the floor. Chess was laughing so hard no sound was coming out. Even Mrs. Carlson was snorting.

Bobby shoved the underpants deep into his pocket. "Static cling," he repeated, but the laughter was drowning him out. "Static cling, static cling, static cling . . ."

The only one in the room who wasn't laughing was Holly. She looked almost as pained as Bobby. Mrs. Carlson finally got the class to calm down by blinking the lights on and off.

Holly stood up. "Bobby Ellis-Chan, I can't believe you would do something like that!" she proclaimed. "Your stunt has nothing to do with the election. It was just a cheap trick to get everyone to remember you."

"But . . . I . . ."

"Mrs. Carlson," Holly said, "may we move on to voting?"

"Yes, I think that's a good idea," Mrs. Carlson said as she dabbed her eyes with a tissue. Bobby, are you done?"

"I'm done," he assured her. "It's over."

During lunch everyone was sporting flag stickers.

"You were brilliant!" Chess declared. "Acting all scared and nervous — and then pulling off that underpants stunt. Now that was a dynamic ending!"

"I was laughing so hard I thought I was going to wet my pants," St. James said. "It was classic."

Bobby smiled weakly. As he poked a hole in his sandwich, Jillian Zarr stomped over to his table.

"Bobby, I can't believe you would stoop that low just to get attention. You made a mockery out of the election. You should be ashamed of yourself!"

"*You* should be ashamed because we're going to win, and the boys will be in charge!" St. James called after her. "Boys rule! Girls drool!"

Jillian Zarr turned around and gave him a look so cold that St. James actually shivered. "For your information," she said, with anger dripping from every word, "Holly will win, the girls will rule, and Bobby will be nothing but a loser!"

The guys laughed nervously as she stomped back to her wolf pack. Bobby pretended to laugh too, but his stomach was churning. The boys were convinced he was going to win. They were counting on him. But what if Jillian Zarr was right?

After lunch, Mrs. Carlson stood by her desk holding a piece of paper folded in half. "I have the results of the election right here."

The class instantly quieted. Holly and Bobby glanced at each other nervously.

"Fourteen votes for Holly," Mrs. Carlson announced. "Fourteen votes for Bobby. It's a tie!"

Jackson raised his hand. "Mrs. Carlson! Mrs. Carlson, it makes sense there would be a tie. There are fourteen boys and fourteen girls in the class."

Everyone but Bobby nodded. It did make sense.

Bobby shook his head in disbelief. It didn't make any sense.

He had voted for Holly.

"Okay, then!" Mrs. Carlson said brightly. "We will now have a run-off. That's what happens when there's a tie. Holly and Bobby, please come to the front of the room. You each can say a little something, and then we will vote again. Bobby, why don't you go first this time?"

Bobby fidgeted as the class stared at him. He checked to make sure there was no underwear stuck to him this time. "Um . . . uh, vote for me" was all he could come up with.

It was Holly's turn. "I promise that if I am elected, I will represent you well at student council meetings." Bobby couldn't help but admire her confidence.

The class did silent reading as one by one students went back to the voting booth. When it was Bobby's turn, he stared at the blank slip of paper. Finally he wrote down a name.

After the last person cast their ballot, Mrs. Carlson quickly tallied up the votes. Then she counted them again to be sure.

"We have another tie!" she announced. A murmur ran through the class. "Room 15 is only allowed one student council representative, so that means Bobby and Holly are going to need to work this out."

Bobby raised his hand. "Mrs. Carlson, can Holly and I talk about this outside?"

To Bobby, being alone with Holly felt both awkward and familiar. They watched Principal Coun hit one of the tetherballs as she crossed the playground. Neither said anything.

Finally Bobby broke the silence. "When did you become a Girl Scout?"

"Just recently," Holly confessed. "It was Mrs. Zarr's idea that we all wear our uniforms today." She adjusted her Girl Scout vest and looked at Bobby. "New suit?"

"Naw, it belongs to Chess." He tugged at his collar. "The underwear wasn't supposed to be part of my speech! It was static cling — honest."

"My mom uses Cling Away," Holly said. "Maybe your dad should try it."

Bobby nodded. "Hey, Holly, thanks for saying I put the underpants on my shirt to get attention. Really, it wasn't planned."

"I know that," she said. "I felt so bad for you."

"Really?"

"Well, yeah!" Holly sounded surprised. "Even though I hate you, I still like you as a frenemy."

"A what?"

"Frenemy. You know, friend plus enemy equals frenemy."

Bobby's ears turned red. "Same here," he admitted. "I even voted for you."

Holly started laughing. "Bobby, I voted for *you*!"

"You did?"

"Well, you looked so miserable clutching Casey's underpants. I thought that for all you went through, you could use an extra vote." Holly took something out of her pocket. "Jillian Zarr wanted me to show this during my speech, but I couldn't do it. Here, you can keep it."

Bobby felt a lump in his throat as he stared at the photo of himself stuck to the Koloff tree. Suddenly he realized what needed to be done.

"Holly, Bobby, have you come to a decision?" Mrs. Carlson asked when they returned to their seats.

Both nodded. Bobby spoke up. His voice was clear and confident. "We have decided that Holly will be the representative for Room 15, and if she can't make a meeting, I will take her place."

When some of the boys booed, Mrs. Carlson shushed them. "The candidates have made their decision and we need to respect that. Congratulations to both Holly and Bobby for being able to work things out. Now, if only we could get our world leaders to follow their example!"

After school, St. James ran up to Bobby. "What happened?" he asked. "Did she threaten you?"

"No." Bobby shook his head.

"Did she bribe you?"

He shook his head again.

St. James looked perplexed. "Well, then, why did you do it?"

The other boys had gathered around by now. Everyone was waiting for his explanation. "Because," Bobby began slowly, "it was the right thing to do."

"Oh, man!" St. James howled. "That's a stupid reason! Geez, Bobby, you blew it!"

★★★ CHAPTER 16 ★★★

Farewell

Bobby rolled up the pant legs of Chess's funeral suit and braced home to see Rover. He couldn't wait to tell him about his horrible speech and the underpants thing. Plus, there was his talk with Holly and the boys being mad at him. Could it have been a more confusing day?

The front door was unlocked. The house was unusually quiet. "Anyone home?" Bobby set his backpack down. "Dad?"

Then he heard sobbing. He could see Casey curled up in a ball on the couch. Tears tumbled down her face, and her crown lay on the floor. Bobby rushed to her side. "Casey, what's the matter?"

She was gulping so much air she couldn't talk. Mr. Ellis-Chan appeared with a glass of water and handed it to Casey. He looked serious. "Bobby," he said slowly. "It was an accident. Rover —"

Before he could finish, Bobby ran up to his room, taking the stairs two at a time.

"Noooooooooooooooo!" he yelled. Rover was floating at the top of the aquarium, surrounded by a cloud of bubbles. "Rover?" Bobby shouted. "Rover!" He picked up the fish food and shook the container. "Rover, look, your favorite! Aw, come on, Rover. Stop playing around. Rover, this isn't funny! Turn over right now!"

Rover didn't move.

Casey was crying so loud it was echoing from downstairs. Mr. Ellis-Chan had followed Bobby upstairs. He grabbed his son and held on tight. "Calm down, calm down. Bobby, please calm down," he pleaded.

Finally, Bobby was tired of shouting. He went limp. As he buried his face in his father's apron, Bobby realized it wasn't Casey who was making the loud crying noises. It was him.

"Rover, Rover, Rover," Bobby sobbed. "Rover." He put both hands over his chest. How could anything so small create a hurt so big? "How?" Bobby asked. His voice shook. "Why?"

Before his father could answer, Bobby spotted something out of place. Next to the aquarium lay an empty bottle of Princess Becky Bubble Bath.

He grabbed the bottle and charged back downstairs to the living room. "How could you?" he demanded.

Casey was sitting on the couch staring at the TV, even though it wasn't on. When she saw her brother, she started crying all over again. Her body was shaking. "I'm sorry, Bobby," she whimpered. "I'm sorry."

Bobby released his grip on the bottle and let it drop to the floor. He slumped onto the other end of the couch. Mr. Ellis-Chan came downstairs and sat between them, hugging Casey with one arm and Bobby with the other.

Later, back in his room, Bobby stared at the aquarium. His father had gotten rid of the bubbles. Rover was gone too.

Bobby's tears felt hot as they ran down his face. His nose was running, but he didn't bother to wipe it. It felt good to cry.

When Bobby finally tried to stop sobbing, he couldn't. To his horror, he started gulping and making weird noises. Then the wheezing began.

★ ★ ★

Mr. Ellis-Chan paced the room as Bobby sat on the couch again, this time wearing his nebulizer mask. No one spoke. Casey was sucking her thumb, something she hadn't done in ages.

The back door slammed shut. "I'm home!" Annie shouted. She barged into the living room, carrying a case of butter toffee peanuts. "I've got to sell these for the football team fund-raiser. Who wants a can?" Annie looked around and frowned. "You guys look miserable. Who died?"

"Rover," her father said.

"That's not even funny," Annie scolded him. When no one said anything, her eyes went from her sister to her brother. "Oh no. Bobby, I am so sorry. Are you okay?"

He shook his head. Mist from his nebulizer escaped and evaporated into the air.

It was almost dark, but no one had bothered to turn on the lights. Instead, Bobby and his sisters and father sat on the couch and stared straight ahead. The nebulizer was off now, and Bobby was breathing normally. Yet he didn't feel normal — he felt numb.

"What are you all doing just sitting here in the dark?" Mrs. Ellis-Chan asked. She set down her briefcase and flipped on the light switch.

"Rover died," Mr. Ellis-Chan said.

"Casey killed him," Bobby added.

"She didn't do it on purpose," Annie explained. "She was trying to give him a bath."

"I'm a bad girl," Casey said. Her lower lip trembled and her normally sparkly eyes were flat. She began to cry.

Mrs. Ellis-Chan rushed over and embraced her. "Oh, honey, you aren't a bad girl. You were trying to help."

"What about me?" Bobby said, rising. "Doesn't anyone care about me? I'm the one who lost Rover."

He ran up to his room before anyone could stop him.

Diver Dave swam up and down, up and down as if looking for his friend. "Rover's gone," Bobby said to him sadly. "He's not coming back."

Bobby crawled into bed without bothering to change his clothes. He pulled the blankets up over himself and held on tight to Mr. Huggums.

★ ★ ★

"Bobby? Bobby, wake up." It was his mother. She was sitting on the side of his bed. Bobby's pillow was wet. "Honey, how about some dinner?"

Bobby couldn't even think about food, but he sat up and let his mother hug him.

"I am so sorry," she said softly. "Rover was really special."

"He was the best pet ever."

"Yes, we all loved Rover and . . ."

"Can we please talk about something else?" Bobby begged. "Anything but Rover."

They sat in silence. Finally, his mom asked, "How was your speech?"

"Casey's Princess Becky underpants were stuck to my shirt."

"Static cling?"

Bobby nodded. He wondered if you could have the worst day of your life twice in one day. "Holly's the student council rep."

"Well, you ran a good campaign, Bobby," Mrs. Ellis-Chan consoled him. "I'm sorry you lost."

"I didn't lose, I won. I mean, I got what I wanted," he tried to explain. "There was a tie. But I knew that Holly would be a much better rep than me, so I let her have it."

"Oh, Bobby," his mother said, kissing him on the top of the head. "I am so proud of you. Rover would be too." She hesitated. "I know I'm not supposed to talk about him, but would you like to have a funeral for Rover?"

His family was waiting in the backyard under the avocado tree when Bobby finally joined them. He was still wearing Chess's funeral suit. When Casey saw him, she hid behind her father.

Bobby knelt down so they were the same height. "It's okay, Casey." Her eyes were red and puffy like his. "I know you were trying to do something nice," he assured her. "It was an accident."

"It was an accident," Casey repeated. She looked like she would burst into tears again. Bobby reached out and gave her a hug. At first she was stiff, but then she hugged him back, and both didn't let go for a long time.

Mr. Ellis-Chan handed his son a shoebox with sparkles and hearts all over it. Bobby knew Rover was inside. "Casey decorated it," he explained. "Would you like to say a few words?"

As Bobby gently cradled the box in his hands, Annie took off her helmet and held it against her heart.

"Rover was the best pet a boy could ever have," Bobby said. Through his tears, it looked like his family was swimming. "I will miss him every day. I love you, Rover, and I'll never forget you."

Everyone was crying.

"I would like some time alone with Rover before we bury him," Bobby said.

Bobby couldn't tell how long he had been outside when the screen door slammed. Casey came toward him, wearing her nightgown. "Here." She handed Wandee to Bobby.

"Where did you find it?" Bobby asked.

"Under your bed where you hide it."

Bobby looked at the wand. "Don't you want to keep Wandee, Casey? I know how much it means to you."

Casey patted his arm. "I just pretended with Wandee. But with Rover, Wandee really was magical. It should be with him."

"Thank you, Casey." Bobby put the wand on top of the box. "Good-bye, Rover," he said. Then Bobby buried Wandee and his fish in the backyard under the stars.

CHAPTER 17

New Friends

The next day after school, Holly came to Bobby's house with a bouquet of daisies. "Your mom told my mom what happened," she said.

"You should have seen everything Rover could do," Bobby told her as they stood over Rover's grave. Bobby had written on a piece of wood:

Holly gently placed the flowers next to the marker. "I'm so sorry, Bobby," she whispered. Her eyes filled with tears.

"Mom and Dad said they'd get me a new fish," Bobby said as they stared at the daisies. "But I don't want another fish. He was my friend, and you can't just go around replacing friends."

Holly nodded in agreement.

The rest of the week slogged by in a haze. Some of the boys still weren't talking to Bobby because of the election, but he hardly noticed. Chess invited him over several times, but Bobby didn't think he could stand seeing Chess and Wilbur playing together.

At home, Bobby mostly stayed in his room. In class, he stared out the window. At recess, he stood off to the side by himself as he watched the boys play handball and the girls roaming in their wolf packs.

"Is that all right with you, Bobby?"

Huh? What had Mrs. Carlson just said?

"Bobby, is that all right?" Mrs. Carlson asked again. She was looking at him like she expected him to say something.

"Um, sure," he said, even though he wasn't sure what he was agreeing to.

Mrs. Carlson held up a paper. "'Rover, the Best Pet Ever,' by Bobby Ellis-Chan," she said aloud.

She was reading Bobby's poem to the entire class? The poem he wrote for creative writing? His private, personal poem? Mrs. Carlson was the only one who was supposed to see it.

If I could have any wish
I would have had a dog, not a fish
But Rover was a special pet
He was as good as you could get
We kept each other company
His tricks filled me with glee
When he died, my heart did break
Even today, it still ache(s)
Rover was a friend
To the very end

No one spoke. No one moved. The silence pushed Bobby farther down into his seat. Right as he was about to hit the floor, an appreciative murmur ran through the class.

Bobby looked up. Mrs. Carlson was holding his poem aloft. It featured a drawing of Rover with wings. Rover was flying through the clouds and smiling as he looked down at the Ellis-Chan house.

St. James leaned toward him. "Bobby, that's a really good picture," he whispered. "You should go pro, like draw comics or something."

Bobby smiled at the thought of it. His heroes, he decided, wouldn't have names like Captain Marvelous and Super Hero Guy. They'd have the names Rover and Bobby.

Someone was trying to muffle the sound of sobbing. When Bobby glanced over at Jillian Zarr, she was staring straight ahead with her hands folded, but there was a tear running down her cheek.

"Has anyone else had a pet who died?" Mrs. Carlson asked the class.

Several kids raised their hands, and so did Mrs. Carlson. As they talked about their pets, Bobby felt happy and sad. He was glad his teacher had read his poem. Rover would have liked that.

At recess, Jillian Zarr tapped Bobby on the shoulder. "I

had a lovebird named Rosalie who died last year," she said softly. "That was a really good poem."

"Thank you —" Bobby started to say.

But Jillian Zarr cut him off. "Your shirt's on backward and inside out again, Bobby. Are you so dumb you don't know how to dress yourself?"

On Saturday, Bobby found an envelope with his name on it next to a plate of hot cinnamon rolls. He picked one up and bit in. The outside of the roll was flaky, and the inside was light and buttery, while the frosting tasted sweet and crunchy with a hint of something familiar Bobby couldn't quite peg. He licked his fingers and opened the envelope.

ROBERT ELLIS-CHAN, MEET ME AT THE CORNER OF FAIR OAKS AND MISSION AT 11 A.M.

There was no signature.

Bobby studied the note. He didn't recognize the writing. Was it from his father or Annie? No, they were at football practice. Chess would just come over instead of leaving a note. What if it was from Jillian Zarr and she was going to slime him with a bucket of bugs? Bobby shuddered at the thought of it. Still, he was curious.

It was possible that the note was from a spy, or maybe a millionaire. One time he saw a TV show about a millionaire who gave money to strangers. This was an exciting thought. He could use a million dollars. "Mom!" Bobby called out. "What time is Casey's dance lesson?"

"Ten thirty," Mrs. Ellis-Chan yelled over *Princess Becky's Planet*.

"Can you take me somewhere while Casey's in class?"

With Casey prancing around in her Petite Princess ballet class, Mrs. Ellis-Chan and Bobby walked to the corner of Fair Oaks and Mission. They passed van Straaten's Sports Closet, the Dinosaur Farm Toy Store, and the Bow Wow Pet Shop.

"Who are we meeting?" his mother asked.

"It's a surprise," Bobby answered.

"Oh! Surprises are nice."

Bobby hoped she was right.

They were standing in front of Yo Cup o' Joe when Holly and her mother strolled past. "Hi, Bobby!" Holly said cheerfully. "What are you doing here?"

"Nothing," Bobby answered.

"Have you been rock hunting lately?"

"Nope," Bobby said. He wished she'd leave. The millionaire might not show up if there were too many people around. Or if he did, Bobby might have to split the money with Holly. He had already decided to buy a donut machine or two, and maybe a skate park, and a new blue yo-yo.

Holly turned to the moms, who were busy chatting about their book club. "Is it okay if Bobby and I go next door?"

Mrs. Harper nodded. Mrs. Ellis-Chan added, "We'll grab a cup of coffee and meet you there."

Holly started toward the Bow Wow Pet Shop. Bobby hesitated. The last place he wanted to go was a pet store.

Besides, he was supposed to meet the mystery millionaire. "I can't go," he said, looking around. "I'm meeting someone."

"I know." Holly laughed. "I wrote the note!"

"You?" Bobby sputtered. "Why?"

"Because you wouldn't go with me to the pet store if I just asked you to."

"Well, I'm not going now." Bobby crossed his arms.

"Don't be silly. I'm getting something for myself, not you," Holly said, fixing her you'd-better-do-what-I-say look on him. "Come with me, Bobby. Please."

Bobby knew there was no arguing with Holly.

Inside the store, Mr. Ed smiled. "Hi, Holly! How's your lizard?"

"Fine, Mr. Ed," she said. "Lulu got loose last week, but my dad found her in one of his shoes."

"And, Bobby, how's Rover?" Mr. Ed asked.

"He died," Bobby said softly.

"I am so sorry," the pet store owner said. Bobby could tell that he really was.

"We're here to get a goldfish," Holly announced.

"What?" Bobby gasped. "I told you I didn't want a new fish!"

"It's not for you," Holly said. "It's for me." She looked at Mr. Ed and explained, "Bobby trained Rover to do all sorts of neat tricks. I want a goldfish that can do that too."

"Follow me!" Mr. Ed said, striding past the puppies and into the fish section of the store.

As Holly and Mr. Ed looked at goldfish, Bobby hung back in the bird aisle. He couldn't bear to look at the puppies or the fish.

Someone tapped him on the shoulder. It was Holly, beaming. "This is Beatrice!" she announced. Holly held up a plastic bag. Inside was a goldfish slightly bigger than Rover. She was white with orange marks.

Bobby choked up. Beatrice was beautiful.

Just then, Mrs. Harper and Mrs. Ellis-Chan came into the store carrying giant cups of coffee. "Mom, look at my fish!" Holly gushed.

Mrs. Harper shook her head. "Holly, honey, you should have asked first."

The smile slipped off Holly's face. "But I can keep Beatrice, right? She doesn't cost that much. I have the money."

"Holly," her mother said in measured tones. "We'd need an aquarium, and those are expensive."

Bobby looked up. He had an empty aquarium. He could give it to Holly — but the thought pained him.

Holly was on the verge of tears. "But, Mommmm, I can't give Beatrice back. She'd be so sad. I'd be so sad."

"I know, sweetheart, but —"

Bobby coughed loudly. "Excuse me!" Everyone turned toward him. Bobby took a deep breath. "What if Holly kept Beatrice at my house? She could live in my aquarium, and Holly could visit her whenever she wanted."

"Really, Bobby?" Holly squeaked. "Pleeeease," she begged her mom.

"Well," Mrs. Harper mused. Holly and Bobby both crossed their fingers. "I don't see why not. If that's okay with the Ellis-Chans."

Bobby and his mother nodded.

"Shall I ring Beatrice up?" Mr. Ed asked.

"No!" Bobby shouted. "Wait. No, not yet." He took another deep breath. "I may want to get a goldfish too," he said, surprising everyone, even himself. "That way Beatrice would have a friend to play with and would never be lonely."

Holly stood by as Bobby took in all of the goldfish in the big aquarium. In one corner, all by itself, was an orange one with brown spots on his stomach. He seemed to be looking back at Bobby.

"That one," Bobby told Mr. Ed.

As Mr. Ed scooped him up and put him in the bag with Beatrice, he asked, "Bobby, does he have a name?"

"Koloff," Bobby said. "His name is Koloff."

Holly turned to Bobby. "That's a great name."

"Thank you," he told her. "And thanks for bringing me here. For Beatrice and Koloff, and for the cinnamon rolls too."

"Cinnamon rolls?" Holly asked. "What cinnamon rolls?"

★★★ CHAPTER 18 ★★★

The Parting Place

WAKE UP!"

Someone was screaming and bashing Bobby over the head with a wand. "Bob-beeeeee, wake up!"

Slowly, Bobby rose up on the bed with a blanket over his head. "I am the ghost of Da-Da-Doo, and I'm going to eat you," he said in his deepest, scariest voice. "Prepare for your doom!"

Casey gasped, then ran screaming down the hall.

Bobby was still laughing as he peeled off his pajamas and put on his jeans. "Well, hello, you two," he said to Beatrice and Koloff. He pulled a static-y sock off the front of his shirt.

"Hey, Squirt," Annie yelled up the stairs. "Get your sorry self to breakfast, NOW!"

"I gotta go," Bobby told them. "But this afternoon we'll start on Rover's famous zig and zag. Meanwhile, practice on your own, okay?"

Bobby sat down and looked at his breakfast — burnt bacon, or maybe it was sausage, and scrambled eggs, or maybe they were potatoes. It was hard to tell. Just then, his dad set a large platter down in the middle of the table.

"Dad, you make the best cinnamon rolls," Bobby said as he reached for one. Annie nodded. Even she couldn't stay grumpy when eating one of The Freezer's cinnamon rolls.

"The frosting's my favorite part," Mrs. Ellis-Chan noted as she licked her fingers. "How did you get it smooth and crunchy and sweet?"

"Butter toffee peanuts," Mr. Ellis-Chan answered. He poured more milk for Casey and gave her another straw, so now she had four in her glass.

"Butter toffee peanuts?" Annie exclaimed. "The ones from my football fund-raiser?"

He nodded. "Well, I did buy that whole case. I crushed them up and mixed them in with the frosting."

"Dad, forget football," Bobby said between bites. "You're going to be famous for your cinnamon rolls!"

After breakfast, Bobby headed toward school. Holly looked surprised when she opened her door. "Do you want to walk with me?" he asked.

Holly lit up. "Sure, I do!"

Both smiled, and then they high-fived with their right hands, high-fived with their left hands, stuck their thumbs in their ears, and wiggled their fingers. "Whoop! Whoop! Whoop!" Bobby and Holly yelled in unison.

"How's Beatrice today?" Holly asked as they started down the street.

"Great," Bobby said. "She's getting really good at flips, and Koloff can almost swim in a circle."

"I'll come by tonight after I do my homework," Holly told him. "Will you tell me what I miss in Mrs. Carlson's class this morning? I have a student council meeting."

"Sure," Bobby answered. "If you save me a donut."

"It's a deal!" Holly exclaimed. She was wearing a new dress. "Hey, did you know that Mrs. Carlson is assigning roles for the class musical today?"

Bobby nodded. "I hope I won't have to sing or dance," he moaned.

"Why? I think it'll be fun."

They quickened their pace when they neared the house with the scary cat.

"Fun?" Bobby asked, as soon as they were safe. "Sure, if you consider torture fun."

The two friends were so busy talking they hardly noticed the Parting Place just up ahead. As they approached, both grew silent. Then, without saying a word, Bobby and Holly kept right on going, together.

fin

This book was edited by Arthur Levine and Cheryl Klein
and designed by Elizabeth B. Parisi, Dan Santat, and
Kristina Iulo. The text was set in Adobe Garamond Pro,
with display type set in Impact. This book was printed
and bound by R. R. Donnelley in Crawfordsville, Indiana.
The production was supervised by Susan Jeffers Casel.
The manufacturing was supervised by Jess White.